RUSTL

Lee turned to stare back over the corralled horse herd to a quick blaze of shooting along the line of the woods. Men yelling.

He dropped the Henry and got up and ran toward the grove, the Bisley Colt's already in his hand. Darker in here—the moonlight dappled by the trees. Behind him as he ran, Lee heard Clevenger shout something and laugh. Rifle fire. They should be able to hold those horsemen. They should certainly be able to hold.

The revolver shooting rippled brightly in front of him again. Crashes of sound. A horse was screaming. Some damn fool had shot a horse.

"Hey, now!" A man calling to him came walking out of the trees.

"Sid?"

"Hell no you son of a bitch!" The man raised a dull-metaled pistol and aimed at Lee as if he were shooting at bottles on a bet.

Lee shot him through the middle and the man sat down suddenly at the report as if the noise had knocked him down.

Lee ran as hard as he could. He crashed into brush, stumbled and slipped to one knee.

A gun went off in his face.

Also in the BUCKSKIN Series:

RIFLE RIVER
GUNSTOCK
PISTOLTOWN
COLT CREEK
GUNSIGHT GAP
TRIGGER SPRING

BUCKSKIN #7

CARTRIDGE COAST

Roy LeBeau

LEISURE BOOKS NEW YORK CITY

A LEISURE BOOK

Published by

Dorchester Publishing Co., Inc.
6 East 39th Street
New York, NY 10016

Printed in the United States of America

BUCKSKIN #7

CARTRIDGE COAST

CHAPTER ONE

When Lee Morgan told them they would be taking the bunch to the rail-head through the Roughs, the boys (meaning Charlie Potts, Sid Sefton, and old Jay Clevenger) were not best pleased.

It would mean a longer ride, though easier on the horses than the high country to the west, less roundabout than a circle out through the Gap and then up to Parker.

The boys didn't care for the route, because the Roughs were not so named for nothing. Those lumpy dips and gullies and broken swales to the north had become in recent years a casual nest of rustlers, homesteaders, plow-jockies, and flatout killers taking a rest from their habitual occupation. Dowd and company, cattle barons and would-be cattle barons out of Canada, were leaving these lands, hundred of square miles of them, to ripen as it were, waiting for the cattle business to recover from that disastrous winter of eighty-six; or, if they proved illusory, for a new flood of monied immigrants to sell the land to bit by bit at a handsome profit.

Meanwhile, claimed only in law, unworked, unguarded, the miles and miles of breaks and brush, steep meadows and steep ravined runs were there for the homeless to settle while they might pending that day when Dowd and company, backed by a squadron of regulators and other hired guns, decided to take possession once again.

It was chancy territory to travel.

So, the boys didn't care for the route, but they let it ride. Lee Morgan, younger than any of them by a year or two, younger than Jay Clevenger by a whole hell of a lot more than that, had none the less earned the job of foreman the hard way—by sweat and smarts, and by tough.

Lean and leathered-down by years in the saddle in all weathers, his dark-blonde hair bleached lighter by the high-mountain sun, with a neat dark-blond mustache, and sun-narrowed eyes the color of amber, Lee Morgan looked to be the saloon-girl's delight, a hard worker—and possibly trouble, considering the Bisley Colt's that rode its holster high on his right hip as if it'd grown there.

And looks, in this case, were not deceiving, as Charlie Potts and the other wranglers could have told anyone who'd asked. Lee Morgan, in fact, *was* a saloon-girl's delight and had been since his half-hour with one years before had pleased her and displeased her beau, a drover named George Peach.

Peach had drawn on young Morgan—nothing but

a kid, then—and had died a few seconds later, victim of a natural fast draw, since considerably refined. That draw had gotten Lee into trouble deep and dark enough to still start memories and rumors stirring years later, trouble that had involved his father—that legendary gunman, Buckskin Frank Leslie—and another, bloodier legend, the murderous leftover from the faded Wild Bunch, Harvey Logan (Kid Curry, to the eartern journalists).

There'd been a shoot-out on Spade Bit, and when the smoke had cleared, both Leslie and Harvey Logan were dead. Lee Morgan, under charges in the shooting of a deputy months earlier, and under some suspicion of having robbed a train as well (Logan had led that robbery, and murdered four men while doing it) was left to try and take his father's place at Spade Bit, doing a good man's work and more, taking a good man's responsibilities and more in the service of Mrs. Catherine Dowd, his dead father's love—and Lee's mother, in all but name.

That work, and that responsibility, the young man had taken on and carried out. Done it well enough so that even Jay Clevenger and Bud Bent, crusty old wranglers who'd shared the post of foreman before Lee came back for good, had had to admit the young man had what it took to labor fourteen-hour days in all weathers, to meet trespassers with fist and rifle and his murderous blacksnake whip, if it came to that.

In the few years that followed, Lee Morgan still proved out, and helped drive the Spade Bit to a place among the best of horse ranches throughout the high-mountain country.

When, therefore, this same Lee Morgan, his stock-chivvying whip coiled at his shoulder like the slim, black snake for which it was named, stood leaning against a mountain sycamore, blowing a cloud of cigar smoke—Grover House Specials—and allowing that they'd drive this particular drive, this special drive, through the Roughs to the rail-head, there was no one present who cared to disagree with him out loud. Charley Potts groaned, but that was the size of the protest.

Lee didn't have to say anything further, but as a good foreman, he'd learned that men do better when they know what and why they're doing it. "I know we'll likely have some trouble up through the Roughs . . ."

Charlie Potts groaned again, and Sid Sefton gave him an elbow to shut him up. The crew was stretched out or hunkered down in a patch of pasture alongside the Little Chicken, taking a short nooner.

"I know that's likely," Lee went on, "but I feel it's worth it, even so. We can get top dollar for these horses—better than the usual top dollar, at that. But only if we get into Oakland first, or damn close to it."

No-one had to be told why California suddenly needed Idaho horses. Spanish fever, in the last three years, had ravaged the California remudas. Now the fever had burned itself out, and horse-hungry California, dealers from Diego to Russian River, were looking for prime working horseflesh and would pay prime prices, in gold, for it.

"So," Lee said, and crushed the stub of his cigar

under his bootheel, "that's why we're going where we're going." He straightened up from the sycamore and walked over to mount his rangy bay, a well-mannered cutting horse named Easy. "Time to go to work," he said, mounted, and led out at a trot, lining for the west ridge. The mares and babies would be green-timing below that ridge, the two and three-year-olds drifting wider, beyond them.

The others stood, and stretched, and spit and farted, then mounted and rode after him. Three good men. Jay Clevenger, gray-haired now, with his reddened beak of a nose and huge mustaches; Sid Sefton, young and handsome, with his Indian-black hair greased and combed to a fare-thee-well; and Charlie Potts, young, tough, and stocky-built, with sandy hair, a merry moon face, and a finger joint missing from his left little finger. (He'd gambled it once, in a barrel-house, against a tin-backed watch and a bottle of Pennsylvania whiskey. He'd lost, but the winner—a San Francisco hoodlum named Byrnes—had let him drink a pint of the whiskey anyway, once the finger joint had been cut off by a quick blow with a Bowie.)

Three fine drovers at the start of their work on Spade Bit—and now, after coddling the ranch's horses for years, three prime wranglers instead. Bud Bent, thickset, gnarled, and strong as a stump, made a fourth hand, and McCorkle the cook more than a fifth, as far as annoyance went.

These men under Lee Morgan with a seasonal hand or two picked up as necessary were for Mrs. Catherine Dowd (somewhat disgraced, and infinitely respected, as the errant wife of Cattle King

Dowd, and erstwhile dearest love of the late and great gunman, Buckskin Frank Leslie) were to her as her family—more specifically, as her children might have been; contrary, quarrelsome, loving, brave, and kind.

For all of these hardworking, rather simple men, Catherine Dowd was an emblem of decent and kind womanhood, a sort of shelter from the ferocity and loneliness of the frontier.

Missus Dowd, and Spade Bit. These were their meadows of home.

Lee saw the others at it, beginning to chivvy the geldings down the first of the long slopes to the headquarters house and holding pens. It would take a good afternoon and evening to drive them to the last ridge; the morning of the next day to drive them down to the flats and in.

Over three hundred of the best—thoroughbred blood in every horse; Morgan blood, too. Solid, quick-starting stock horses, the finest range stock in Idaho. Any one of them, with good care, could carry a man the whole three thousand miles across the United States, lug a man from Oregon to the coast of Maine, if that was his pleasure. And do that on grass, too, if grain was too dear for him. Any of them could do thirty, forty miles a day, regular as clocks. Something less on grass, of course, but still get a man where he wanted to go.

And if a sold animal afterward proved to have a flaw—bent wind, a tendency to sprung tendons, fragile hooves—then the buyer could come on out with the animal and make his case. Mrs. Dowd had refunded money on seventeen horses, that Lee knew of. Seventeen, out of more than two thousand sold over the years. Solid stock, and known to be for a thousand miles and more, east and west, north and south. High-mountain stock, with strong quarters and deep lungs.

There was a fair market value of over ten thousand dollars in these three hundred geldings alone—make that fifteen to twenty thousand in the California market, now. A good deal of money, even for prime stock. Enough money to make the wild ones scattered through the Roughs sit up and take notice. And if a hard-case couldn't get up a gumption or a big enough bunch of allies to hit for the main herd, well, just one Spade Bit pony cut out on a rainy night would give an owl-hooter a priceless advantage—a fast, staying horse, almost sure to be better conformed, more fit to run than almost any mount, and thus any rider, that he was liable to come up against.

Well worth a try, most of them would figure.

Lee intended to discourage that sort of figuring, before the drive. They'd have trouble anyway, of course, but he might be able to cut it down some.

He reined the bay north, aiming just off the massive granite shoulder of the Old Man, where the great mountain towered, wearing bright spring greens along the timber lines . . . the spring snows, at higher elevations. Lee aimed just off the mountain's shoulder into the scrub breaks beyond the north pastures.

Had been some time since Spade Bit had had trouble with the scum of the Roughs. Lee and the Bit crew, and old Shand of Broken Iron, had led altogether twenty-six men up there two years before. The ranchers had ridden in with pine pitch torches, stockwhips, and a hangman's noose. They hadn't used the noose, though in more than one case they might have, finding Broken Iron hides here, a Spade Bit mare with a clumsy altered brand there.

They'd whipped. They'd burned. But they'd killed no-one.

"Next time," Lee Morgan had told the Bergenreich brothers, "next time, I'll hang you both, and any other horse thief we find."

The brothers, both hairy and burly as bears, lived in rough log shacks with an assortment of women and children—a number of those children gotten on others of their children, so the stories ran. The Burgenreichs were not particular about that sort of thing. There were also stories that they were cannibals, too, when the mood and opportunity struck. Not unheard of in these deep mountains, and occasionally without the excuse of winter snows and starvation.

Lee had told them, then had his men tie one of the brothers to a tree, and had lashed the hulking brute until the man had howled like a wolf in his agony and finally fainted.

"You'd not do such to me, if not for these men," the other brother had said then, seeing it was his turn. He had a fairly thick Dutchy accent.

Lee had tossed his whip to Bud Bent, then his Bisley Colt's—the same model his father's had been—to Sid Sefton, and had taken a running jump onto Klaus Bergenreich.

It was a manner of fighting his men had seen Lee

use before and was just the opposite of the usual stand-off-and-slug-the-fellow-down style favored by most ranch people.

Lee jumped up onto Burgenreich like a pissed painter onto a hunting dog, and, perched there high on the brute's broad shoulders, gripped his hair in one hand and struck the man in the face very hard and very fast with the other, raking his back and sides with Spanish spurs all the while.

Burgenreich had howled and snarled and bucked and reached up thick hands to grasp and pull Lee down. Lee, still balanced atop the man, had seized one of those groping hands, and broken first one finger, then another, snapping the bones in half like green-wood sticks.

Then, leaning out and over as the big man spun, staggering, trying to dislodge him, Lee Morgan had neatly put a thumb into Burgenreich's left eye, driving his thumbnail deep into the soft of the eyeball.

And, with this done, and the big man groaning, stumbling with shock, Lee had slid off and away from him as he would have done off a half-whipped cayuse, turned again to face him, and kicked Bergenreich in the stones—full swinging kick behind the pointed toe of his riding boot.

The big man, hurt past screaming, had silently doubled up and fallen to his knees and Lee, taking his time now, had set himself, stepped in, and swung a long round-house right in to strike the fellow alongside his mouth and break his jaw.

Lee and his men had ridden away a few moments later, leaving one of the brothers still moaning on the whipping tree, the other silent in the dirt. A number of women and children had watched the whole show with great interest, standing huddled in a row just beneath the rickety porch of the cabin which the Burgenreiches had built high onto a muddy bank.

The women—black haired, big cheekboned, most of them, full of Indian blood—had made neither yelp nor squeak during the beatings. Nor had they seemed pleased to see the brothers receive something of what they often handed out. They only watched without expression.

The children had done the same—except for one small girl, who had hidden her face in her hands.

Oddly, it was that little girl that Lee remembered when he had occasion to recall that fight. She'd been a slender child, her arms and legs as thin as lathes. He could recall very clearly her standing with the rest, the others watching as open-eyed and dumb as owls, but she, her slight shoulders hunched, her face buried in thin hands as her father was beaten so cruelly.

It shamed Lee to remember her.

Too pleased with himself, sometimes . . . Too pleased to frighten other men and set them down . . .

Something to be careful of.

And even so, the men of the Roughs needed that lesson, and now could use another. Spade Bit was doing well—as, for that matter, was the small horse ranch Lee owned at Rifle River, five hundred miles away. That ranch was run by Tom Cooke and Jake

Sandburg, old friends and partners. Spade Bit was doing well, but not well enough to stand the loss of a herd of more than three hundred of their best horses. Not well enough to stand the loss of half that number. The hard-cases of the Roughs would have to be reminded to stay clear of that drive.

He guided the bay down into a grassy swale, and spurred him to a canter. Time to put in a first installment of that warning, and to have some pleasure in the doing.

Phil Surtees had moved into the north Roughs some three years before with some cash in gold, thought by most to be the proceeds of a robbery in Texas. Surtees was a Texican, and had the reputation of being a dangerous man—not, perhaps in face to face encounters, of which he seemed a little shy, but almost certainly in encounters of another kind, ambushes and dry-gulching, back-shooting and barn-burning. For this reason, his small cattle run, too small to be called a proper ranch, had been largely left alone by the other outcasts of the Roughs. Surtees was not a man to cross unless you had eyes in the back of your head.

Within a year of his settling and buying his eight hundred acres along the upper *Gros Ventre*, Surtees had stolen sufficient stock from Broken Iron and the other cattle spreads to set himself up as a cattle feeder and breeder for market.

He'd been visited now and again by Sheriff Meagher—and by cattlemen and their drovers—and had managed to hide his stolen beeves in time (warned by the Roughs' swift exchange of rumor) to avoid a beating, or arrest, or a hanging from his own stable beam.

Then he had stolen or received as stolen goods four horses from the Spade Bit.

A month to the day after those animals had appeared on his place and without any Spade Bit people come calling in vain, these same four horses disappeared from Surtees' pastures. And with them, seven other animals—in fact, every horse Surtees had on his place. Surtees had been wakened to this theft by the glow cast against a midnight sky as his barn went up in flames.

When the confusion was over and Surtees, still in his nightshirt, had finished surveying his ruined barn, realized the loss of all his riding stock, and gone back to his slab-side cabin to put on his trousers, he found a printed note pinned neatly to his pillow:

"TWO EYES FOR AN EYE," it said, and was signed by a simple drawing of a spade bit.

Spade Bit lost no more horses to Phil Surtees and, after the beating of the Burgenreich brothers, lost no more stock to any of the hard-cases in the Roughs. The word was out. *Lee Morgan was foreman of Spade Bit. His father had been Buckskin Frank Leslie and the son favored his father, had killed two or more to prove it. Leave the Bit alone.*

And so they had—until this coming drive. That would be a temptation too great to withstand, unless a small reminder was administered. And even then, over three hundred of the finest working horses in the West might be too juicy a target to pass up.

The long swale had given way to broken ground, the choppy grass-filled gullies, scrub patches, and sudden rises that marked the Roughs. It was poor thin-soiled country, too poor for profitable stock raising on a large scale unless by an outfit big enough and rich enough to haul in winter feed when needed.

Sheep, maybe, Lee thought. Might be able to raise some sheep up here . . . Hadn't been many sheep in the valley in the years since his father and Frank Pace had shot it out in the Grover House. That fight had determined who was going to rule this section of the country—sheep, or cattle. Pace had died in that fight, as had the leader of the sheepmen, and the land past Gunsight Gap had been beef land ever since.

Still—the Roughs might be damn good sheep country. It had the look. Could be over-grazed, of course, if the herders got greedy . . .

Lee smiled to himself as he rode. Had been a time that just *thinking* about running sheep with cattle or horses could have got a man called out. But now, with the open range closing down fast, it was beginning to seem good business to use every foot of land to its best advantage.

He'd think about the sheep when this drive and sale were over. Might be these Roughs could be put to some use better than as corn-crib farms and hard-scrabble fit-outs for men on the run.

He might go on up to Canada . . . talk to old Dowd about it.

The riding got rougher as the land steepened, breaking, rising up onto foothills and sudden canyons, and Lee had to mind the bay's footing on steep gravel washes, sudden briar-snarled banks. Hard riding, but for the weather. The weather was prime and would remain prime, with luck, for the drive. Hot, clear-skied late spring—or, if you preferred, early summer. Perfect weather to move stock, especially as they were to be trailing no young ones along.

Lee turned in the saddle as the bay single-footed along a ridge line, and looked west at the mountains, the Old Man and his brothers, the high *cordillera* of the Rockies marching away west, peak after peak, snow still shining on their crests. Prime weather . . . prime country. High mountain country. The best, Lee thought. The best anywhere.

He reached Phil Surtees' spread almost an hour later. It was a level length of acreage in fair bunch grass, bordered on one side by a branch of the Ventre, on the other by a wind-stunted stand of pin oak.

Lee rode on down the meadows, scattering an occasional bunch of bony cattle and noticing the blurred Rocking-S burned into their hides, usually, but not always, covering another brand. Rustled stock or the get of rustled stock and no doubt about it. Lee had heard that the Montana ranchers, the big ones, were hiring gunmen to run the bust-out stock raisers off the range. Just such men as Surtees. Seeing this spread, it was hard to blame them.

Halfway down the stretch of grass—most of Surtees' eight-hundred acres, Lee supposed—he saw two horsemen quartering toward him half a mile away, ridden out of a bunch of oaks.

Lee pulled up the bay and sat waiting for them to ride up to him. It was a useful thing that Bud Bent had taught him—sit your horse and rest him, and let strangers tire theirs riding up. Then, if there was trouble, a man had a slight edge, running or chasing.

Lee sat and only eased his gunbelt around a bit so that, sitting, he could reach the butt of the Bisley Colt's a little quicker.

He watched to see if either of the riders coming in had a rifle out and ready and was leaning forward to slide the Winchester out of its scabbard, when he saw that both riders had their hands showing and empty. He sat back and relaxed, letting the reins slip so the bay could mouth some grass.

It took a while for the riders to come up, and Lee recognized Surtees, riding the near side and mounted on a tall chestnut. He didn't know the other man—a big man with a big belly, mounted on a thick-legged black.

The bunch grass was deeper here, and the riders' horses had to high-step it. A nice action on the chestnut; the black looked lucky just to be able to carry his load. The big man on him was wearing a Mexican hat, one of their wide brimmed wool *sombreros.* Looked to have a pair of guns in *buscadero* holsters, too.

And, watching that fellow as they rode up (a dark face on him fierce enough to stop a pendulum clock) it appeared to Lee that Surtees might have recruited a fellow to back him in face-to-face matters.

"What in hell are you doin' on my land, Morgan?" Shouted out, and not in Surtees' usual style at all. Lee supposed he was right about Big-belly in the Mexican hat.

They came up to him in a hoof-thudding and trampling on grass, leather squeaks, and the jingle of bit chains. Big-belly at once swung his horse to come around at Lee's other side so they'd have him between them but Lee spurred the bay and reined him left, then pulled him up on the other side of Surtees' chestnut, leaving Big-belly out on a limb.

"I asked you a question, Morgan!" Surtees said, breathing as if he'd been doing the running and not his horse.

Surtees was a tall man, strong and stoop-shouldered, with pale hair, milk blue eyes, and a sheep's long nosed face. He looked up to all the rigs, and some tough, when first seen. But on encountering the milk blue eyes and finding them shifting away, men tended to change their judgment of him. Surtees wore a Deak & Sommers .44 revolver, a large double actioned weapon, in a plain holster well down on his right thigh. It looked handy enough for a pull-and-shoot.

"I came up for a neighborly visit, Phil," Lee said, glancing past Surtees to see what Big-belly was up to. Big-belly was staring back, looking considerable tough. He was fatted-up hard, like a good sized black bear, and was dark complected as an Indian, including a set of narrow eyes dark as dark water. He looked a very strong man, but perhaps not too quick. " . . . Just wanted to have a little talk about Spade Bit's drive."

"What drive?" Surtees said, already lying. He'd known about the coming horse-run for sure—would have heard about it in town, would have heard that the Bit was rounding up its three- and four-year-olds.

"What are you lookin' at, Pretty Boy?"

Seems that Belly didn't care for being looked over.

"I was just glancing at a fat-gut asshole," Lee said, leaning forward in his saddle to give the Belly a friendly smile. "You take exception to that? If you do, why, you can just reach for one of those irons, unless you have shit for a backbone."

Now, the Belly was big enough and looked tough enough to keep most men careful in his presence, but Lee had learned some time ago that it was wiser with some men to push them before they got set to push you. And also, he had, at an early age, met some truly dangerous men . . . some extraordinarily dangerous men. An insane Iroquois giant, for one, who would have eaten poor Big-belly for breakfast, and two other men as well who would have made nothing at all of that same giant Iroquois.

When a young man's been scared by Harvey Logan and saved by Buckskin Frank Leslie, well, the memory makes most hard-cases look pretty soft.

"Well . . . ?" Lee watched Big-belly, waiting to see if he had anything further to say or do. He was looking past Surtees, but could see him well enough to notice any sudden movement.

The man in the Mexican hat sat glowering and said nothing. But, give him credit, he didn't seem to be pissing in terror, either.

Lee sat back in his saddle and relaxed.

"The drive we're running," he said to Surtees. "I've come up here to warn you off it."

"Now, God damnit . . ."

"Oh, shut your mouth, you yellow dog—I'm tired of your noise and postures. You're a damn thief, and that's well known! If you or friends of yours come out after that herd, I'll run you down and kill you."

That seemed plain enough talking. Perhaps too plain for Surtees to take, at least with another man listening, for the tall man reached down and put his hand on the butt of his Philadelphia pistol.

Lee leaned over toward him, lifted his arm, and swung the shot weighted butt of his quirt as Surtees' head. The scrub rancher, still not decided on his draw—his reach being more a demonstration for form's sake—had to decide at once whether to duck and pull his revolver, or duck and not pull his revolver.

He took too long to decide, and ducked too late.

The leather-wrapped handle of the crop caught him fairly alongside his head with a loud hard cracking sound, and he stiffened in his high cantle saddle like a shot rabbit. As his Stetson fell off his head, he toppled slowly after it, making a muttering sound, as if he were trying to speak. He fell off his horse to the far side, away from Lee, and Lee watched as he went, looking past to see if Big-belly wished to take a hand.

Big-belly did not. He sat as stolid as a stump aboard his thick-legged black, and watched Surtees pitch sideways and down into the grass.

Surtees landed with a soft *thump,* the grass

cushioning his fall a great deal. Big-belly watched, then glanced up at Lee and said, "Foot's caught in the stirrup." Meaning that the chesnut, already restless, might bolt and drag the unconscious man to his death.

"Catch the horse up, then," Lee said, and kept his eye on him. Big-belly was a cooler customer than he looked, and bore watching.

Belly caught up the chestnut's reins, and he and Lee sat their horses without speaking for a while. Lee was waiting for Surtees to come to himself.

Surtees lay curled in the deep grass like a large ugly child, asleep but restless. Soon, after a minute or two, he groaned, rolled to his side, and opened his eyes, staring up at the sky.

"What say, Phil?" Lee said. "Have a headache, do you?"

Surtees blinked his eyes, raised his head to stare up at Lee, then cursed. Slowly got to his hands and knees, grunted with effort, and stood up, staggering a foot or two to his left side. His face was white as fine flour, and he looked ill.

"You hearing me all right there, Phil?"

"I hear you . . ." Surtees stopped talking and cleared his throat. He looked around for his hat and didn't see it. It was on the grass behind him.

"You recall what I said about that horse drive, don't you?"

"I recall you . . ." Surtees gagged, and had to stand silent for a moment. "I recall it—and I'll never forget it." He had a bad look on his face, which was as red now as it had been white.

"And you'll stay clear of our horses?"

"I'll . . ." There were tears of rage in the tall man's eyes. "Oh—I swear I'll kill you for this . . . !" His face was beet red now, and he was weeping.

"But you'll stay clear of our horses."

Big-belly sat his black, and said not a word.

Surtees shook his head, weeping. "No," he said. "*I won't do anything you say!*"

More to the man than Lee had thought. Which, in a way, was too bad.

Lee spurred the bay right at him—as sudden as that—and as Surtees stumbled back from the horse's driving shoulder, Lee reached down swinging, and hit him with the butt of the quirt again.

It struck Surtees across the back of his head, and the blow pitched him down into the grass on his face.

Lee booted the bay into a rearing turn and saw that Surtees' friend had still not made a move. Big-belly was doing the rustler no good at all today.

Surtees, stretched out full length, called out something and struggled, thrashing in the deep bunch grass. Looked to be drowning down there.

It was hard doings, to knock a man silly once and then again. But better than killing him, Lee thought. A beating had calmed the Bergenreiches; might do the same for this thief as well.

Surtees, coming awake sooner than before, hunched up like an injured animal and managed to get to his hands and knees. There, he stayed a while, his head hanging down. There was no blood on his head where he'd been hit.

He stayed that way for a while, then said, "Charlie . . ." and vomited what looked to have been a considerable dinner into the grass.

Lee assumed Big-belly was "Charlie."

"You want to get down, give him a hand?" Lee said. But the man in the Mexican hat just shook his head, and sat his horse watching both of them.

Once he'd vomited, Surtees appeared to feel better, and he sat down in the grass and took some deep breaths. He said something, but it was hard to make out.

"What did you say?" Lee said. But Surtees didn't appear to hear him.

Lee walked the bay over to him, and Surtees looked up and looked frightened of being hit again. It was getting on late afternoon now; the sun cast their shadows long across the grass.

"Will you stay clear of our horses?" Lee said.

Surtees stared up at him from where he was sitting in the grass—he'd put his left hand down in his vomit.

"Yes . . ." he said. "I won't . . . I won't do anything." Saying that appeared to tire him, and he lay down on his side, but still held his head up in an awkward way, staring up at Lee. The sun was in Surtees' eyes; he had to squint. He had vomit on the sleeve of his checkered shirt.

The lesson was given then, and Lee felt near as sick with it as Surtees. Striking the man that second time had been poor doings . . .

But better this than a night raid a week from now,

and horses missing and good men killed. Some of the Roughs might try for the herd even so; likely would —but Surtees was a clever man; raiders would be disadvantaged without him.

Worth a do-and-try, in any case.

"Don't forget, now," Lee said, and glanced again at the man in the Mexican hat—not wary of a sneak draw, Lee'd kept his still shadow well in sight—but curious. There was something to the fellow, no doubt about it; once backed down, he'd stayed backed, and hadn't shifted or blustered about it, simply kept an eye on Lee, as if to see what else he was made of.

Big-belly was something of a thinker, then, and that was something to keep in mind.

"Good afternoon," Lee said to the man, and touched his hat. Big-belly, no expression on his face at all, returned the courtesy.

"Good afternoon," he said. And as Lee turned his bay to ride away east, grunted with the effort and swung his massive bulk out of the saddle.

He stood beside his horse's head for almost a minute watching the Spade Bit foreman go—unconcerned, apparently, about a try at a back-shot. "Well," the big man said softly, "you're a dandy young dasher, and quick. And little damn good it's goin' to do you." Then, grunting again, he bent, gripped Surtees under his arms, and heaved him to his feet.

"Phil Surtees," the big man said, his dark face still, the Indian blood showing, "you are the damndest fool of a partner I've ever suffered."

Surtees clung to him, trying to keep his balance.
"And," the big man went on, "you're getting your dinner on my shirt."

CHAPTER TWO

LEE rode east another four miles, then cut down a narrow canyon to his left, ducking as the bay shoved through a stretch of woods, the overhanging pin oak branches scraping at them as they forced through. The woods smelled of green and fresh growth, and were so thickly laced that twice Lee had to turn the bay aside to find clearer going.

The bay broke out into a wildflower meadow running down a steep slope to another tangle. Lee reined the horse to the forest edge, then rode along it, skirting the thickest of the growth. Even sheep would have their work cut out to eat this country open. Goats might be a better notion. Lee grinned to himself at the picture of the boys at the Black Ace in Grover welcoming goatherds to the bar.

Be a novelty.

A hedge of wild plum barred the way into the next open run, and Lee rode up to it, gave it a look-see, then backed the bay off, took a short run, and jumped the hedge with a foot of air under the horse's belly. Not bad, for a working horse with a working saddle on his back—not bad at all.

The sun was well down now; the shadows ran like wide black ribbons over the grass and rough scrub. In one of these shadows thrown by a bigger oak than most Lee pulled up to rest the bay, and to wait a while and see whether Surtees or his bulky friend had had a mind to follow in chance of a lucky shot.

Lee took a cigar stub from his saddle-bag, slid off the bay's back, and leaned against the oak's trunk to ease himself, to blow a cloud, and to listen for someone coming rattling through the thickets.

Larks were flying out of the meadow grass a stone's throw off speeding straight up into the sky, singing so brightly it seemed it was the singing kept them up in the air. A pretty day, it had been. And due, perhaps, to get prettier, if he was in luck, and Surtees and his friend stayed out on the range rather than riding for home to poultice Surtees' aching head.

Was an Academy professor, once, Professor Riles out in Cree County, had told Lee that men would fly just like the birds some day. He'd said that some Frenchmen were already working to build flying machines. Hard to see, watching those swift climbing birds, so small and sure, just what sort of a machine might bear a man up into the air with that speed. Though it would surely be something to see tried . . .

Lee finished his cigar, turned to the tree trunk for a satisfactory piss, then walked out to catch the bay up and mount him. It seemed that neither Surtees nor his careful friend had chosen to follow Lee along and perhaps do him harm. Might be that caution would extend to Spade Bit's horse drive a week from now.

Lee spurred the bay on east, down along the line of forest to the north-south run of a small creek, unnamed, as far as Lee knew. "I'm calling you 'Lark Run,' " he said, as the bay splashed over it, and then kept on at a steady trot toward a thin intermittent drift of wood smoke not half a mile away.

Surtees had built his cabin down in a scrub oak swale alongside the ox bow course of the new-named run. The cabin—big enough to be called a house, in this country—had a parlor floor with an inside kitchen behind it, and two bedrooms in a second story. Those, and a long front porch, made it fancy doings. Very fancy, for the Roughs.

Lee pulled up in a clump to the south of the house where he could see the barn to the right, the corrals to the left. The barn was raw-wood new, rebuilt from the burning. There was stock in the corrals, four or five good enough horses. Not Spade Bit stock, though.

Lee sat his saddle, watching for a while. The bay, restless, tossed his head now and again, smelling grain from the barn.

After a few minutes, Lee saw something moving around the side of the house. Looked closer, and saw it was Susannah's skirt—some light blue stuff, with polkadots, it looked like—shifting as she tended a line full of drying clothes. She'd walk out from behind the house to pin up this or that, then walk back out of sight, following the length of the line, he supposed.

A dog was barking 'round the back there, probably scented the bay, maybe Lee's cigar smoke as well. Shy dog, though, wasn't coming out front to see . . .

Lee touched the bay with his spurs, and the big gelding headed up for the house at a trot. They recrossed "Lark Run," and Lee reined the horse around the side of the house.

The woman had heard the hoofbeats by then—the dog barking louder, too—and looked up from her basket of wash as Lee trotted the bay into the backyard. She looked a little wary (as well she might, a woman left alone at a ranch in the Roughs) then saw who it was.

"Afternoon to you, Sue," Lee said, pulled the bay up and swung down off him.

Susannah Surtees favored her brother but not too much. She was a tall, bony, freckled woman, with mild blue eyes and a long nose. The small, light brown freckles covering her face and arms like spatters of brown ink made her look more of a girl than she was, for Susannah was thirty-six or seven if she was a day. If her eyes and height were her brother's, her silence was not. Susannah Surtees had little to say.

"Hello," she said to Lee, not seeming surprised, though he had not been up into the Roughs to see her for some months. And she said nothing more, but stood by her basket of washing, looking at him.

Her stooped shoulders, the large, bony hands clutching a wet pair of jean trousers were those of any ranch woman near worn out with work. There was nothing to her that seemed out of the ordinary, to look at. The nasty reputation that had gathered concerning her appeared unlikely to anyone meeting her at the Surtees house. She kept that house for her brother. Had been married to a man named Luffold, it was said. She worked her turn and more, as did all women on the frontier, was nearly plain (with years and freckles) and had, in short, nothing remarkable about her . . . rumored a fairly poor cook.

But she was randy as a rabbit.

So the tale had been told some years before by two brothers, drifting drovers named Packman, who had worked a summer for Surtees, and, in Grover afterwards, preparing to ride back to Wyoming, had claimed to have fucked the woman in her brother's house, in an upstairs bedroom, the two of them together.

This had been news indeed, and was reinforced by further gossip from the Roughs, that a rustler and gunman named Charley Storm had had the woman, too, taking her out of her house while Surtees was out droving, and screwing her on a horse blanket in the wood lot out back.

Word, after that, was that the woman would go with almost anyone who happened by, and loved it. This unlikely-looking Jezebel, as one or more of the Grover ladies called her, was supposed to have spread herself open for a party of five men. Storm and some others, on another occasion—this out in the wood lot also—and let them look as they pleased, then take their turns with her, and Susannah Surtees all the while gasping and thrashing like a hooked trout, her long, naked legs sometimes wrapped around the man at her, sometimes splayed wide, as if to show what was being done to her.

It was assumed, of course, that Surtees knew of all this—could hardly not have known—and, for some reason (shyness being one) did not choose to object, or to call men out.

Lee had heard the stories and not paid them much heed. His business with Surtees had been horse business, and stealing business, and punishing business. Not personal, with the man's womenfolk. Still, he'd heard the stories, and, riding up on the sly to see how thoroughly Surtees' barn had burned that time ago, had come upon Susannah out back, hoeing in her kitchen garden.

He had talked to her, seeing as he did the ruin of the barn, then (nothing ventured, nothing gained) had spoken in a friendly way, and standing near her, had put his hand on her shoulder—bony, with softness between the bones. Susannah had made no protest to that, hardly had seemed to notice the touch, in fact. So, in a slow and gentle way much as he if he were calming a restive horse, Lee had patted and stroked gently along her arm—long, and wire-muscled, and traced with fine blue veins.

Susannah Surtees had made no sign of unease, and Lee had gently cupped her breast, small, soft, and sagging slightly with its meagre weight.

The woman had not protested. Had stood patiently while he massaged and felt of her, rolling the soft nipple in his fingers, gathering her breast in a handful beneath the soft cotton of her dress.

After a while of this, Lee had gripped her by the back of her neck, and holding her that way, had walked her back into her house, through the kitchen to a narrow parlor with a hooked rug on its floor, and had pushed her down onto her face on a home-made horse-hair sofa, pushed her skirts well up, spread her legs and then her naked privates well apart and, as she grunted with it, thrust his stiff cock up and into her, finding her as hairy, wet, and needing as the talk had had it.

Lee had been ashamed, afterwards, to have burned a man's barn, then tupped his sister in his house—but he'd been young enough, too, to feel some proud of what he'd done there, and that he'd pleased the woman so that she'd bit her knuckles and cried out with the pleasure of it.

Since that time, Lee had had Susannah Surtees more than once, drifting by the rancher's house whenever he rode up into the Roughs to see that no Spade Bit stock had drifted or been drifted so far north. When, as sometimes was the case, Surtees and his two or three hands were out on his small range shifting beeves from here to there, Lee had taken advantage of that.

He supposed that Surtees suspected it and didn't care.

"Saw Phil up on the west hundred," Lee said, and tied the bay off to a chicken coop leg beside the back door. Better have the horse handy, he thought. Surtees might still take a notion to trail him east.

Susannah watched him and said nothing, then

turned awway to pin up the trousers on her line, stretching to get them high. Lee saw her freckled naked ankles, the sturdy work shoes she wore.

Lee watched her pin the trousers onto the line, then one of her brother's shirts. When she was finished with that, Lee said, "You come on in the house, now." And Susannah Surtees, as obedient as a bitch dog, turned from her washing, bent to pick up a sock had fallen in the dirt, shook it clean and put it back in her wash basket, and went on up the back steps ahead of him and through the kitchen door.

She kept Surtees' house well. The kitchen, the hallway, the stairs up to the second floor, were all as smart and shining as a Dutch woman's house might be, the plain pine floor scrubbed and sanded to a fare-thee-well.

The bedroom she led him to was whitewashed, the small bed against the wall made up in sewn flour sack sheets, washed thin, and bleached white as the flour they'd held. There was a fine, bead-worked elk hide on the bed as a cover, and Susannah Surtees picked it up and rolled it carefully, so as not to hurt the lie of the hair on it, and set it on the floor beneath the window.

She was breathing loud enough for Lee to hear as she carefully turned the bed sheets down. "You have to take off your boots," she said.

"I'm taking off every damn stitch," Lee said, "and so are you."

She stared at him, pale lashes, pale eyes.

"No," she said. "I have my curse . . ."

Lee paused while pulling off a boot, and damned

his luck. "Have you then?" he said. "And what will you do?"

She put a forefinger to her lips as if wanting him to be quiet. She held her finger to her lips for a moment, then put out her tongue and touched it.

He wanted more from her than that.

"Yes, you'll give it a fine sucking," he said to her. "And you'll take off your clothes as well. I know what you've got, and I'll have a look at it."

She stood silent, apparently thinking about that, then slowly began to undress, reaching behind her back to undo her buttons.

Lee was naked in a few moments, his gun belt on the washstand by the bed, and stood watching her. His cock was up, swollen red and vein-knotted.

Susannah took off her dress, tugging it awkwardly up over her head, took off a flour sack underthing and a petticoat of some blue cloth. Then she untied the band that supported her breasts, reached down to take off her heavy work shoes, and reached up to take a faded red bandanna scarf from her pale braids. She stood before him naked in the warm yellow light of late afternoon, with the dark ginger hair at her crotch half covered with a small roll of white cloth, held in place with two narrow strips of fabric—one up between her legs, the other attached to the ends of that cloth, circling her waist like a belt. The small roll of cloth was stained and spotted with dark red and light red.

It was the first time Lee had ever seen a woman revealing herself in such a fix, and he stepped over to her, reaching out, and ran his hand along the strips of cloth that made up the rig.

"Don't," she said, "that's all nasty," and put her hands down to try and stop him from touching there.

Lee brushed her hands aside, held her by her hips, and bent to smell at her. In her period, she smelled like salted meat at a summer camp, rich, and sweet, and spoiling.

"That's all right," Lee said, and leaned forward and kissed her belly. "There's nothing wrong with that."

He stood up, took her by the arm, and led her over to the bed. He pushed her down on it, and while she put her hands up and tried to stop him, Lee pulled and tugged the cloth bands off her, and took the roll of cotton from between her legs. Wisps of hair at her crotch were stained and stuck together with blood, but Lee tossed the cloth onto the floor, held her to the bed, and reached down and put his hand on her.

He squeezed the sticky, damp fur gently, and slid a finger up into her with a soft, kissing sound.

"Oh, dear . . ." she said. "Oh, dear!" And twisted over on her back and spread her thighs wide apart. She craned her neck to stare down at herself as he moved his finger inside her, slippery, and hot. When he pulled his finger out, it was red with blood.

"Ah, you started me again," she said, and put her hand down on his to stop him from doing that. Lee, kneeling on the bed over her, roughly pushed her hand away and put his hands on her again. He slid his fingers up into her, into the wetness and heat, feeling the dampness of her hair there against the back of his hands as he worked and spread her cunt, gently opening it, forcing it wider, pushing his fingers deeper into her.

"You're making me bleed!" she called out as if she were going to cry, but her hips twisted and thrust up against his fingers. Blood was smeared across the white, freckled skin of her thighs. She began to grunt as he worked in her, her hands fluttering up to squeeze at her breasts, to pinch and tug her nipples.

Susannah drew up her knees, clamped her long thighs to Lee's hand for a moment—then, as he drove his fingers deeper into her, gasped, and spraddled her legs wide, stretching herself open for his hand.

Lee pulled his hand away; she was wide open, deep, and bloody as an ax wound. The curdled smell of blood rose from her.

Lee, afterward, could never understand why he'd done it but then, bending over her, smeared with her, smelling her, feeling the slipperiness, the smoothness of her skin, hearing her grunts, her moans as he took his hand from her, licking at the blood, the juices of her, sucking, biting gently, lapping at her like a starving dog, shoving his face against her there to get deeper, to get more of her, more of the trembling blood-slick meat of her.

Susannah Surtees drew in a breath and shouted, and thrashed under him so desperately that Lee almost lost his grip on her hip, her buttocks. Then, still driving his face against her, working his tongue into her, he slid his right hand from her hip, down and around and up the warm crease of her ass as she kicked and struggled, searched, and found the small dimple of her asshole and slowly pushed a finger up into her there.

The woman yelped beneath him, and bucked as the finger drove into her. Then he felt her fingers in his hair, tugging, hauling his face harder against her. She twisted, and her long legs kicked the air on either side of his nodding head.

"*You're killing meeee . . .!*"

Holding her down now with one hand pressing at her belly, the other still at her ass, Lee slowly raised up . . . took his face away from her, took his hand from her belly, reached down to place himself, and thrust the full swollen length of his cock into her.

It went up into her like a steam train, and Susannah Surtees howled with the pleasure of it.

Lee lunged against her, reaching up with his free hand to grip her hair, hold her still as she twisted and struggled beneath him. She was silent, now, wrestling with him for the pleasure she wanted—more and more of it. Lee felt the soaked heat of her cunt deeper into her. "Oh, you're killing me . . . oh, Mister, you're killing me . . . !"

Lee stared down into her pale, sweating face, contorted as if he were sliding a knife into her instead of an instrument of pleasure. She groaned as he pulled it almost out, then thrust deep into her again. Lee wanted to get higher, to ride her higher; he slowly slid his finger out of her ass, and she gasped. Then he leaned high over her, gripped her hard with both hands, one at the back of her neck, one at a soft breast, and began to drive and drive into her as she grunted beneath him, shuddering with the impacts as they came together in sounds of smacking flesh.

Lee felt it starting, felt the sweet, growing pain of it—pleasure so sharp, it hurt. He moved and moved on her, staring down into Susannah's face. She was turning her head from side to side, blind with it, the freckles stood out against her white skin like spatters of ink. Then as he thrust into her another stroke, Lee saw a slow flush of red rise up from her sweaty shoulders, and on up into her throat, her face . . . until, thrashing, bucking, grunting her delight, and blushing like a schoolgirl, Susannah Surtees opened her eyes, stared up at him, and came to her time, weeping and shouting.

Lee fucked into her just once more all the way, gritted his teeth, and moaning with pleasure, with the aching pleasure of it, spurted into her. Deep . . . deep . . . all the way.

They lay together after that for a little while, gasping . . . exhausted, slippery with their sweat, the jissom that slicked her long pale thighs, the dark red streaks of blood at her groin, the soft hair between her legs clotted red.

After a while, though, she moved under him, and Lee, supporting himself on trembling arms, climbed up and off of her and stood naked—and reached to a chair back for her dress. She who a few moments before had seemed like some pagan goddess to Lee, all gaping cunt, squeezing thighs, her mouth open to scream out for joy, now looked like any tired ranch woman put upon by thoughtless men.

"Thank you, Susannah," Lee said, reaching for

his own clothes, now. *Thank you for such a personal thing, such a wonderful thing,* he wanted to say. But he didn't.

Susannah Surtees didn't look at him, and didn't answer him, either. She got dressed while he did, then she sat back down on the bed to rebraid her hair.

It was dusk and near dark when Lee rode out of the last of the Roughs, heading the big bay south, down the first of the long ridge slopes back onto Spade Bit land.

Quite the fellow, he might have thought—beat a man and screw his sister, and all in an afternoon. Quite the fellow . . . but there was mighty little joy in it, as far as swelling his head went. For the one thing, Susannah Surtees had given him more of a gift than he might have expected. It pleased him just to remember it. Nothing to strut about there—taking advantage of a poor loose woman, couldn't help herself, and had the name for that all through the country. But what a pleasuring she'd given him!

And for the second thing, beating Surtees had been no hero's doings. Fellow was known to be shy, at least face to face. Shy, and slow of hand. No. No hero's doings.

A fool's doings, in a way.

Because Susannah had given him a glass of buttermilk in the kitchen (damn fool to linger and stay for it, of course, a kid's risk-taking). She'd given him his buttermilk, turned her cheek away from a thank-you kiss, and told him Phil had a new partner—fellow named Charlie Packwood. Some

Cherokee blood there, and a very mean and cruel man.

"Mexican hat?" Lee asked, just to be certain sure.

And yes indeedy, a Mexican hat.

So young Mister Smarty-pants had upped and whipped the wrong partner in that lash-up while the dangerous one sat and looked him over.

"And since when had Phil had any damn partner?"

Susannah was washing his milk glass in a pan of water. "Phil played cards with Mister Packwood in Boise three weeks ago." Mister Packwood had won the hand that counted, and had come right down to the place to claim his goods: a one-half interest in the ranch. Had come down, and had stayed.

Phil not caring for it above half, and if the big-bellied man was as smart as he seemed, he'd watch his back from now on. Phil not caring for it, but scared to brace the man face to face. And Susannah? Lee didn't ask her, didn't know how to ask her, really, if the man was taking advantage of her being here in the house with him . . . taking advantage of Phil's cowardice to do as he pleased with her. Hadn't young Lee Morgan, the terror of the countryside, just done the same?

Pretty damn close to it.

For that reason, then, and for making a fool of himself before Packwood—old Big-belly would damn sure come after the horse herd; no matter to him if his shy partner had blubbered and said he wouldn't—Lee had a pleasureful screwing to remember, but nothing much to be proud of. He thought of his father sometimes, when he'd done this or that . . .

wondering what the old man would have thought of it.

He knew damn well what Frank Leslie would have thought of today's doings, the screwing to the side. He'd have thought Lee'd played the ass up on Surtees' meadow.

And he'd have been right.

There was a line of choke-cherry bushes down the track. Lee, more to change his subject of thinking than shorten the ride, put the big bay to them at a canter and leaned forward as the horse left the ground in a nice, stretching jump. Cleared the things like a feather floating.

The brush behind him and his gut a little bruised by the saddle horn—work-rigs weren't built for horse-jumping—Lee reined the big horse across a steep pasture and then down into a shallow creek bed. No water in the thing. Never had been, as far as Lee knew.

A good distance down that, then up and out of it and the long climb to the last ridge over headquarters. Would take him an hour and more, almost two, and he'd be riding under moonlight the last one. Would come into headquarters over the edge of the ridge, and then down the last long stretch through the pine grove . . . and home.

Pine grove. He'd stop there, have a word . . . as he'd done now many times. Just in case the dead could hear a living man, or cared to listen . . .

As far as Lee knew (and he *would* likely have known) none of the hands had told any tales about the burying of Buckskin Frank Leslie. And there'd been a considerable tale to tell.

Damned good men. Spade Bit men, every one. And of course, they loved Catherine Dowd. Wouldn't be wanting folks to think her a fool . . .

They'd buried the man in a small clearing, up in the pine groves behind headquarters. Catherine Dowd had wanted him buried in that grove; wanted him buried in that small clearing there, too. A man, if he was alive and standing up, could see the peaks of the Rockies through the pines. That place seemed to mean something to Mrs. Dowd, and she'd wanted Lee's father there, and that was where they'd buried him.

That evening had been hell. Lee walking around the place—one round fired from that old Remington he'd been so proud to sport—walking around the place as dead inside as a cigar store Indian. And Mrs. Dowd driving up the lane in the buckboard, and Lee having to tell her, because there was no other person on the place to do it except for McCorkle the cook, and he was down at the south corral gate crying like a baby.

Lee'd told her but almost hadn't had to. She'd seen him standing by the house porch, and seen his face, and had pulled up the horses beside him, and sat looking at him for a moment.

"*Frank.*" she said. And said nothing more, only sat and stared at Lee while he spilled the thing out like vomit. Catherine Dowd had looked exceptionally beautiful that day. She'd had a fine white dress on, with lace around her throat. And she'd had a duster on over than that. A long white duster. And a straw bonnet with a ribbon on it. The color of the ribbon was all that Lee couldn't remember, when he remembered her sitting up on the buckboard, looking at him.

He'd told her. About Harvey Logan. The fight in the cook-shack.

He'd told her Frank Leslie was dead.

She'd looked at him and heard him out, and then she'd gotten down out of the buggy, said, "Bring him in to me," and had gone up the steps and into the house, her back as straight as an army officer's.

Lee and McCorkle had gone to get Frank Leslie and they'd carried him into the house.

Catherine Dowd was standing in the bedroom, waiting for them. She watched them put Lee's father on the bed and then waited until they turned around and left her alone with him.

Two of the hands rode in just then, Bud Bent and Sid Sefton, and it had to be told to them as well. Lee was tired of telling it.

After the sheriff had come and gone, and some of the neighbors, and the undertaker and two deputies had come for Logan's body to take to town and put on show, and then hold for the Pinkertons to look at and make sure it was him for sure . . . After all that, and a moonless night that lasted way too long, they buried Buckskin Frank Leslie in the early sunlight of morning.

Lee and Ray Clevenger, Charlie Potts and Bud Bent carried the plain pine coffin out and up to the grove. Sid Sefton helped them up the steep part of the track. McCorkle had worked through the night carpentering the coffin out of fine-cured red cedar he'd been saving for an outside kitchen table.

The coffin lid was off. McCorkle carried that

himself. So they could see the dead man lying on a bright folded quilt, looking as natural as if he'd just fallen asleep alongside a trail. Mrs. Dowd had dressed Frank Leslie for a long ride, in denim trousers and polished boots, a good checked wool shirt, green and black, a red neckerchief knotted at his throat, and his Stetson tilted down over his face, as if to shade his eyes for a long sleep. A fine sheep-skin coat was rolled beneath his head, and Catherine had strapped his gun-belt on, the Bisley Colt's oiled and loaded in its holster. In the dead man's right boot-top, his double-edged Arkansas toothpick rested, the knife sharpened keen as a Swedish razor.

There was a two quart canteen, fresh filled, at his other side.

The hands noticed these things, and exchanged looks as they did, but no one said a word.

They put the coffin down beside the fresh dug grave at the center of the sunny clearing and then stood waiting for Catherine Dowd to tell them what to do.

She was wearing black, like a legal widow, and was dressed, even in that sad color, like the finest lady, her long hair—once all rich brown, now laced with fine strands of gray—combed up and pinned beneath a hat and veil as black as night.

It struck Lee, and maybe one or two of the others, that Mrs. Dowd had had widow's clothes by her for some time, as if to be ready for Leslie's death from his terrible wounds before, when he'd first come to her, or from this newer injury she must have expected from whatever source.

Catherine Dowd, looking down at the love of her

life and the loss of him, had never been lovelier, though her face was white as marble stone.

She stood over the coffin, looking down and suddenly said, "*Frank . . . ?*" as if to be certain he was surely dead and not sleeping. Then she bent low in a rustle of black silk, and kissed his mouth, shadowed by the brim of the tilted Stetson, stood up and said, "Cover him, Tom."

McCorkle fitted the lid on then and nailed it down.

Catherine Dowd looked at Lee and waited.

Lee went to the coffin, put his hand on it, and said, "Good-bye, Father." Then he turned to the men and said, "Put the coffin in there; I'll bury him."

And they did, and left the grove, and Lee Morgan, with his father's lover watching, took the shovel, and buried Buckskin Frank Leslie.

The next afternoon Mrs. Dowd had the hands dig a deeper, wider grave just below Leslie's, and while they were doing it, she went to the stables, picked Dandy—a fine, big-barreled roan—had him tacked out, put Leslie's saddle on him, and strapped saddlebags loaded with spare ammunition, jerky, coffee, salt and sugar, cigars, a match safe, and slab of bacon behind the cantle. Then she tied a yellow slicker to the saddle straps, and slid Leslie's big Sharps rifle into the boot.

The men had just finished digging this other grave at the foot of Frank Leslie's and were leaning on their shovels, talking about it, when Catherine Dowd came up into the grove leading Dandy.

Lee, leaning against a pine smoking a hand-rolled, had had his own notions what the bigger grave was to be for, and was not surprised to see Mrs. Dowd come up with the horse. She led the animal up alongside the edge of the pit, patted its glossy neck, and murmured something to it. Then she took a small nickel-plated pistol from the pocket of her dress, put the muzzle to the horse's ear, and fired a shot into its brain.

It took the men a while to fill that grave, and to exchange looks of a kind while doing it. A horse, a dead horse, for a dead man to ride . . .

"More Indian doin's than white folks'," Bent said, later, when he and Ray Clevenger were out chousing stray geldings in, "but I see the notion behind it . . ."

Clevenger had had nothing to say, and although Dandy had been one of the best animals on the place, especially for a ride of distance, none of the other men had much to say about such oddity and likely waste either. None of them had had anything at all to say about it in Grover, and the town knew nothing of it, then or later.

It was regarded as Spade Bit business, Catherine Dowd's business.

Perhaps Buckskin Frank Leslie's business.

Lee rode down into the grove well after dark, riding slow and careful by moonlight. He could see the lamp light at headquarters below, hear someone calling—likely McCorkle cussing a hand for not scraping his dinner plate into the slop bucket.

Lee guided the bay down between the tall pines, the horse's hooves silent on pine straw. A night wind was getting up, breezing softly through the moonlit green, drifting the scent of the pines into

Lee's face as he walked the bay down, the big horse weary under him, its fine stride gone stiff and jolting.

At the clearing—seeming larger now, in moonlight—Lee swung down and led the bay over to his father's grave. He stood there for a while, looking at the slight mound of earth carpeted now with fallen pine needles—and, at its head, looming pale in the silver light, the tombstone Catherine Dowd had had carved and freighted in from all the way from Boise. And on the rough granite, carved in letters shadowed deep enough to read even in that light

HERE LIES FRANK LESLIE
"BUCKSKIN"
THE BEST THERE EVER WAS

Lee stood listening to the wind, seeing his father . . . seeing him standing in the dirt beside the old corral, looking up at a son he hardly knew . . . seeing a son ready to ride away forever . . .

"Listen," his father had said, "if you get into a tight . . . then you come back here. You come straight back here—and we'll stand together."

He said it, and had meant it. And had died, getting it done.

"Daddy," Lee said, softly, as though his dead father had the ears of an owl or a fox, "I surely played the fool today and it's going to cost us, down the line. This Packwood fellow . . ." It sounded like a deal of whining to Lee, to be saying such small things, to be complaining like a child to his dead father—and about a thing like Packwood, nothing but a sharper and saloon bully by the look of him. Frank Leslie would have done Big-belly for lunch and hardly noticed the doing.

Standing silent in the moonlight, looking down at his father's grave, Lee wondered if the old man's dreams—if dead people dreamed—were restless with the memories of men he'd killed. Marshal Phipps, in Cree, and some big Irish rustler before Phipps . . . some Russky foreigners, supposedly, and a gunman named Shannon or Shane, said himself to have been the gun that put down Slim Wilson, out of Cheyenne. Those men killed, and the Lord only knew how many before that, when he was bartending in Dodge and friends with Holliday and that crowd. Then, Tombstone. Then, the stories went, had killed two hard-case brothers, the Bothwell boys, and—it was funny—supposed to have killed a man named Peach, same name as the wrangler Lee had shot to death. Strange thing, for father and son both to have killed men named the same . . .

The Coe brothers . . . Lee'd heard of the Coe brothers. His father had killed them in terrible fights, first one, then the other. And another man, too.

And Pace, of course.

And Harvey Logan. He had killed Kid Curry to save Lee.

It seemed to Lee that weight of dead men would tell on Buckskin Frank Leslie, even in the grave. Had certainly told on him, alive. There'd been a sadness about his father . . .

"Well, forget it, Daddy," Lee said softly to the night. "I'll get her herd driven through. " He turned to mount the bay and paused, his boot in the stirrup. "I'll keep taking care of her for you."

He mounted and reined the bay on down the slope, past the long, larger mound where the horse Dandy, shoed and tacked out and loaded for a journey, lay at his father's feet.

Lee let the bay take his own easy pace down and out of the grove, away from the soft sounds of the night wind through the pines.

CHAPTER THREE

TEN days later, they pulled out.

A new man named Crossman, Bud Bent who was getting the least way gnarly for a drive, and the cook, McCorkle, were left behind to watch the place, tend stock, and take care of Catherine Dowd. The neighbors and especially the Robinsons, who had two hard-fisted boys had been asked to be on the watch as far as Spade Bit was concerned, and Sheriff Meagher had said he'd have his deputy, Donnervliet, stop by from time to time.

For the rest—Charlie Potts, Ray Clevenger, Sid Sefton, another new drover named Ford (a silent, slight little man, the size of a jockey) and Lee Morgan as boss—they lined out with 342 of the best working ranch horses, gelded, fit, and fine, to be seen in the West, and herded them up and over the north ridge just as dawn edged past the Old Man.

Mrs. Dowd had driven up to gather-camp for a

dark-hour breakfast to say goodbye, and found them already eating. Lee'd made room for her beside him on a fallen pine log, and Sefton'd gone and gotten her a plate of red beans and bacon from McCorkle's wagon—a last courtesy to the drovers, since the chuck-wagon wouldn't be going along. It would be fry-pan fixings here on out.

Catherine Dowd was a woman of appetite, lady or not, and she'd dug right in to do justice to the beans. "Lee," she'd said between bites, "why not run further west? I'll take a chance on a broken hoof or two, rather than those rascals." By which she meant the people in the Roughs.

Lee had put his tin plate down in the dirt, pulled his belt knife, a wide-bladed double-edge fashioned from a buck saw blade, and reached down to draw her a map with the point.

"We go far west, Mother," he said, "and if they *do* come and have sense to come that far, and *push*, they'll have us sided up against canyons, and they'll drive us into them. Once we're in there, the herd'll have split a dozen ways . . ."

He sat back up, wiped the knife blade on his pants, and sheathed the weapon. "We'd lose more than seventy head, I think, if they did that." He bent again to pick up his breakfast plate. "I'd a whole lot rather lose ten or twenty in a running fight." He began to eat.

Catherine Dowd said nothing for a few moments, thinking about that, and watching Lee out of the corner of her eye, fiddling with her food the while. She saw the memory of his father in him; the back of his neck, his hands—his hands were his father's to the life, long-fingered, big-knuckled . . . gentle.

Lee turned to look at her. Eyes nothing like Frank Leslie's—these amber, intent, fierce as a bobcat's eyes. Not that remembered cool gray.

"Be careful, son," she said. *Careful.* As well talk "careful" to the wind, or to a young mustang stallion in the mountains.

Lee smiled at her. "I will. I don't aim to be shot by a horse thief."

Catherine Dowd remembered the first time she had seen Leslie alone. He'd been practicing with his pistol . . . standing on a sunny slope, lean, intent, neat in scrubbed blue denims, with a young man's body and the face of a man who'd seen it all, a lined, weathered face, graying mustache. And the smooth elegance of his reach for the revolver—as smooth and swift, she'd thought, watching, as the neat circles machinery made in pursuit of its task. The shots had come cracking, booming across the field, and something—a peach can, she thought—had gone leaping, jumping, bouncing along as if it were alive.

Catherine Dowd had thought little of guns, and less of the men, so common in the west, who sported and boasted of them. This was, she saw, the original article, something special, beyond the pistol on his hip.

He had been smiling as he shot as though standing beside himself and finding his own extraordinary skill something odd, almost ridiculous. Watching him, she had not fallen in love, certainly not then, and most certainly not with his skill at pistol shooting. But perhaps she had prepared herself to fall in love, to care deeply for such an odd man . . . such a quietly humorous man.

Later, she had not been surprised to learn his real name. Not surprised that he had killed many men, was famous throughout the entire country as a man killer, murderous with a knife or gun.

She had not been surprised. But it had made her sad for she understood how much it had saddened him.

"Your father," she said suddenly to Lee, saying it as she dug her fork into a slice of bacon, not looking at him, "your father had a pistol draw as smooth as a peeled boiled egg." She looked up at Lee then. He was listening, eating. "Your father told me that a man with corners to his draw was always slower than he might be."

Lee listened, then looked up at her, smiling. "I said I'd be careful," he said, leaned over and kissed her cheek, then stood up and called across the camp. "Saaay, now! Hop it up! Let's get trailin'!"

He strode away from her without looking back, rousting the hands, joshing McCorkle about his beans, getting the fit-out ready to travel. The sky was lightening in the east, beginning to dim the sharp circle of shadow and light the campfire made. Mrs. Dowd watched him move amongst the men, the horses, moving as lightly, as powerfully as a young horse himself.

"*A fitting son, Frank,*" she said to her man, now dead and gone. *A fitting son.*

By noon, they were high on the north ridge. A few

miles more, riding higher, and they'd be in the Roughs.

The herd was strung out a mile and more, no harm and no danger now in such open country. Lee had set Charlie Potts to ride point with his rifle across his saddle-bow. Sefton and Clevenger to side the horse herd, and Ford to bring up, leading their one pack pony. Lee rode widdershins, where he pleased or was needed, keeping the mass of lively geldings on notice that a man rode here and there around them as they traveled, and was already in sight.

Lee'd pushed the herd hard this first morning. He wanted the edge off the horses; wanted them too tired, too calm to go stampeding if some rustlers took to firing off their revolvers in the night, or galloping in out of the afternoon sun hallooing and waving blankets.

The day was bright and fine, the sky one clear sheet of blue with no clouds to it, not even out to the west, over the first peaks of the Rockies' cordillera. A wind came down from the mountains, though, a strong steady wind with the smell of snow still on it. Strong enough to lift the wranglers' Stetson brims as they rode, to stir the buckskin fringe at the hem of Lee's jacket, ruffle his horse's mane. Lee was riding a horse called Popeye, a stocky pinto with a walled right eye that looked blind but wasn't. Popeye was not a fast horse particularly, but he was strong as a Short-horn bull, and very neat on his feet. A good mount, Lee thought, for quick work on rough country.

He reined the pinto over to the left, edging down a

grassy slope through a tangle of scrub, keeping even with the horses filing past at a slow trot. He looked the herd over, watching for trouble—a laggard, or a limper. A big, late-cut black named Diablo was leading out like a stallion, leading just fine. Clevenger had wanted to bring Martha, the Bit's bell-mare, to lead, but that would have meant having to sell her in California or ship her back by rail lonesome. Martha being something of a pet on the place, that was decided against.

"That big-nuts," Clevenger had said, referring to Diablo, though the black had lost his testicles, if only lately, "That big-nuts was always trouble, an' always will be!" The black had dumped Clevenger two years before, likely producing this harsh judgment against him. "A damn bad horse, an' they never fix!"

Ray had been running the colt out in the breaking ring, and the black colt, with a twist and a jump, had run Clevenger out instead, dumped him, then turned and rushed old Ray under the fence planks for his life. There'd been an amused audience.

But Ray'd been wrong. The big black horse, late broken and later gelded (he'd loned it for a season up in the foothills, well past the start-spring of the Little Chicken) was leading fine. Lee wasn't sure that ol' Martha could have kept ahead of such strong young horses on a fast dive over harsh country.

Lee pulled the pinto and sat the saddle at ease, watching the slow river of horse flesh, browns and blacks, bays, grays and pintos, sorrels, chestnuts and three or four whites, as they trotted in bunches and strings, singly and crowded, up the narrow under slope of the ridge. The late spring sun shone on their hides as if each young horse, full of strength and stay, had been covered neatly with a coat of fine satin or silk, this color or that.

They raised no dust in the deep shagged grass, but a steady rumble of hoofbeats, neighing, snorts as they moved a little up, dropped a little back, and whickered amongst themselves some sort of recognition.

No dust. But Lee didn't fool himself that the herd went unseen, unknown.

It had been seen, for sure. And it was known.

Today, tonight, they'd likely be left alone—might not have been interfered with at all, if only he'd had the sense to brace Packwood and if necessary, put him down, instead of wasting time with that shy fool of a Surtees.

Bad judgement. And it was going to cost.

In the first few years he'd taken on the running of Spade Bit, Lee'd often considered himself too young and foolish for the responsibility. But he'd learned fast, and had perhaps been too proud of himself for the learning. His smarts, his whip, his gun. With those, he'd missed making mistakes or corrected any mistakes, he'd made, regardless.

Or so he'd thought. And so the country all around seemed to think.

Now, sitting Popeye, watching the herd that might, for value, be a torrent of gold, Lee wondered how much he'd been playing the fool all along. Considering it, he could hardly remember any ranch question coming up that Catherine Dowd hadn't been there to talk over with him, calming him, helping him to a judgment that would stand for months and years, not just for a piece of a season, not just for admiring looks at the stores and livery when next he rode to town.

And if trouble came, he'd had the hands. Hard cases, every one, and Spade Bit loyal to the bone. They hadn't mixed in, of course, most times. Hadn't had to, he realized now. Their presence, shadowy, always there in the back of every possible quarrel . . . How many men had backed off a fight with Spade Bit's young foreman because of the Spade Bit men, the Spade Bit name . . . ?

It made unpleasant considering.

They didn't noon, but drove the herd on—now well into the Roughs, the make-an'-breaks, some used to call them before Dowd came into the country, when a desperate man with a rope and running iron might cut himself a starter herd of beeves and no one the wiser—or if they were, prepared to do anything about it. What were left of these men now were the poor riskers, the slow, the vicious, the stupid. The clever ones had made their small piles, seen how the wind was blowing toward the rich land corporations and had skedaddled.

Lee was riding up close to point now, with Sid Sefton having taken over from Potts. Sefton, dark, sleek, and handsome, had been a brave boy not afraid to try conclusions with Ben Thompson, once (and had survived that by great good fortune, Thompson's drunkeness, and the courage of Catherine Dowd) and now had grown into a very tough young man, wise and quick and dangerous. It puzzled Lee occasionally that Sid didn't pull stakes and head for some new country, to try for a place, a fortune of his own. But it seemed that Sefton'd already spent too many good years on the Bit, sunk his roots deep into this Rocky Mountain range—and his John Thomas into more than a few local ranch and farm girls, if rumor was right—lived too much of a sweet life here to want to pull up and leave.

For that matter, Lee himself could have up and gone back to Cree and Rifle River, or to Chicago, for that matter—been offered a chance at the beef slaughter business there.

Sefton was off to the right, just a little ahead, just a little to the right of the lead horse in the herd—Diablo, trotting along like a railroad locomotive, sleek black hide gleaming in the bright mountain sunlight. Lee noticed that the big black didn't shy off scrub and go around the way most horses would have. Diablo plowed on through like a boulder rolling.

Sefton was moving faster, riding further out and further right. The herd was throwing dust now, not much, but enough for Lee to see Sid riding a quarter mile away in a haze of dust white as placer sand. He could see the glint of sunlight on Sefton's rifle, one of the lever action Winchesters. A gift, that had been . . . Mrs. Dowd.

Spurring the pinto up and over the breast of a gamma grassed swale, Lee thought a bit of how Packwood and the others might go about hitting this fine herd for stock . . .

Thought how *he'd* do it, were it up to him to plan the way.

He glanced to the right, and saw that the bunch behind the lead were lagging. There was a gray there, and a sorrel, didn't care for bucking brush as Diablo did.

Lee reined Popeye over right, reached down to the blacksnake coiled at his saddle-bow, freed it, and shook out the whip's slender black lash. More than fifteen feet of fine narrow braided leather, black as night, and tough as telegraph wire. Lee shook out the coils and began to swing the lash in great hissing circles over his head as he rode.

Popeye's ears went up and back, then set forward again as he went about his business of avoiding chuck holes and dog holes and gopher holes while keeping up a spanking pace over horse-break country.

Lee swung the pinto in closer to the herd—saw a bunch of soft green leaves at a cholla elbow, tucked his wrist as the whip hummed above him, turned his forearm, and brought the lash whining down—hauled back on the handle as a sailor might on a boat's oar in rough seas, and the cholla branch was splintered with a rifle's crack. The leaves floated through the air like feathers, and, far away, Sid Sefton turned his head to see that Lee was at his whip practice, and had not fired a shot.

The laggard gray stepped it up, the sorrel following. The whole bunch stepped neatly out as Lee rode in still closer on their left, the blacksnake lash once more hissing above his head, swinging in perfect, blurred circles.

A meadow-sweet blossom, wind-blown in high grass as Lee passed and swung the lash and sent a long, long loop, like a wave of leather, rolling down to the loaded tip.

Again, that high, stinging, ringing crack. The lovely meadow-sweet, its head lifted off like a pretty French girl's by the guillotine, now blew in the wind as another stem of grass.

The bunch near the point moved faster still at that second explosion, and Lee spurred Popeye alongside the running horses and let the whip speak for him again.

Now they lined out, the gelding running as straight as mares, light-footing it over the country. Far to the right, a little ahead, Sid turned in his saddle to wave. The sun shone on his rifle's barrel again as he moved.

Lee turned in his own saddle, looking back. Through the dust, the colors and movement of the horses, he could barely make out little Ford tracking down a slope a half mile back, the pack horse, a thick-belly named Pete, stumping along behind.

Lee pulled Popeye in a bit and let the pinto ride off left, out of the noise and rush of the horse herd. He rode the pinto's slowing pace into his jolting trot, coiled the blacksnake and hung it at his saddle bow.

He knew now, or thought he did, what Packwood was likely to take a try at.

It was what Lee would do, in his place. Well—one of two ways. The first rustle (and least likely) would be a try at the horses before night. Today, when the herd was hardly into the Roughs. Spade Bit wouldn't be expecting a try so soon, so near home range.

That would be a good go. Costly, but probably a

surprise . . . probably get some twenty or thirty head, maybe more, if the hands could be driven off . . . If Packwood had got enough men together. . .

That was one way.

But there was a better.

Hit the herd tonight and seem to hit it hard. Make this appear to be the try . . . even lose some fools riding in. Then next morning, at dawn when the Spade Bit men would be still slapping each other on the back for being such dandy fine shooters—then come for real. Come killing. And take the horses after.

Lee thought that that was what he would do, were he in Packwood's place. And, remembering the man's cool and considering ways, he thought Packwood would be at least that smart, and maybe smarter. Might be able to figure a way Lee couldn't counter. But no use pouring sweat about that. "Do your damndest, and then fuck it!" Philosophy of McCorkle, ranch cook.

So be it, then. Prime the men that Packwood—Packwood for sure—Lee rode at a resting walk, remembering the bulky dark man, his Mexican hat, the fancy *buscadero* gunbelt, his slow, thoughtful ways—prime the men that the herd would be hit, and likely tonight. Hit hard but not for long and the rustlers driven away easy, or fairly so.

Then, tomorrow at dawn, the humdinger, the real thunderhead would come rolling, and it would be make or break, shoot to hit or go right under.

Men killed? His men? Spade Bit people?

For certain sure, if the Roughs meant to have thousands and thousands of dollar's worth of the finest saddle stock bred. Men killed on both sides, for certain sure.

Lee booted the pinto with the stirrup sides, refusing his spurs, and the stocky gelding grunted, lifted his head from a fresh bunch of buffalo grass, and paced right up into his jarring trot as if he'd never heard of a range horse grazing on a working occasion. Sefton had drifted nearer; forking a long-striding dun called Ace, Sid never had to strain to stay ahead of a bunch of anything. On the Bit, it was first up and out and quickest with his rope got the ride of choice, but still, Ace was felt to be Sid's ride, even when he was slow crawling out of his soogins and into the frigid five o'clock dark. Sid had petted the horse and doctored him and fussed over him and spoiled him since the big dun was a colt. Had offered to buy the beast, too, but Mrs. Dowd wouldn't have it. No private-owned horses worked on the Bit. A rule with good reasons, and that was that.

Still a fine mount, and worked like two horses for Sid, a return for all that coddling.

Lee figured his camp as he rode. Someplace sheltered, near water, where the horses could be tree-roped, so as not to stampede when the shooting started. If the shooting started . . .

"*If* there's any damn shootin'!" Ray Clevenger stomped around the coffee fire like a barnyard rooster on the prod. "You're tellin' me this here's a notion and that's all it is?"

"It's what I'd do, Ray."

"Jesus H. Christ, boy! These horses haven't had but a drink of water! They have to graze, Lee

—they gotta be loose to graze. Don't, an' you're goin' to trail some mighty sad stock up to Parker, boy!"

Out behind the old ranny as he stomped and argued, the horses shifted restlessly, the geldings packed close into a grove of dwarf birch turned into a huge, hasty corral by the hands' lariats, uncoiled and tied tree trunk to tree trunk to enclose almost two acres of grove. Where the ropes wouldn't reach, Lee'd had the hands cut saplings for barriers and split rails. It was mighty rough, and a horse or two might break out in a scramble, but not the whole herd. The herd was in. And staying in.

"They stay in, Ray. If I'm wrong, we slack 'em out in the morning."

Clevenger stopped stomping, and stared Lee hard in the eyes; his long gray mustaches seemed to bristle and quiver like a cat's whiskers. "You fool with these horses, now, like this, you're goin' to rub the edge right off 'em. It's goin' to cost the Bit some money come to sale, I can tell you that! These animals still gotta do a railroad train ride!"

"Better than having them stolen." Lee could sense the other hands listening to the old rooster stand up to the young stud duck.

"Shit, Lee," Clevenger said. "You really believe any of that Roughs trash is going to come in here and *fight* us? They might try some poor sneaky . . ."

"I think they'll fight."

"Shit. That Surtees is yellow as a fice dog an' the rest of 'em is scrapin's, and nothin' more."

"I saw a man up there was no dog. And the rest of those people are desperate for cash money—*and* good horses. I don't think they *can't* fight us for this herd, many as they can get."

"Shit!"

"They can't come down into the range after them. They've got to make a try up here. And I believe they will."

"Well, hell's bells, boy . . ." Clevenger was half convinced. "Well . . . hell, we can whip those people! No need to tie the horses down."

"We can drive off their first try, I agree. But I think they'll come again, after—a big bunch. And the stock had better be penned then, or we'll lose 'em."

Clevenger sighed and stomped a give-up stomp. "All right, then. You do what you think best, boy. But I'll just say this—this is a trick you can't pull more than once on trailin' stock; these horses just won't bear it, bein' squeezed in like that, hardly able to draw a breath, and no damn grazin' for a day and a night. You damn well *better* leave 'em loose in the mornin'!"

"Soon as the shooting's over, Ray."

Clevenger called to the others over his shoulder. "This damn boy's as goddamn stubborn as a boar badger!" The hands laughed, relieved to see no serious argument, and went about their business.

"Say, Ford," Lee called, "break out that bacon, and bust some cold biscuits in a pan. We'll have a fry." The little man nodded, and went to the horse-pack for the fixings. "Coffee, too, and we'll take some of Potts' red-eye!" Charlie Potts, reknotting a length of rope round a fat bole tree, an exception in this grove of young timber, made a face.

"You will like hell!" he said.

"We will like anything," said Sefton, bringing in an armload of firewood. It was no secret that Charlie Potts, jolly as ever and a tough boy, had none-the-less something eating at him from time to time that he soothed with a canteen full of poor whiskey from the Union or the Black Ace in town. In such a small crew of men who'd worked with and known each other for years, there were few secrets. Charlie had been unable to keep his whiskey secret for any time at all. And in the Spade Bit fashion, it had been accepted kindly enough, since he never drank sufficient to spoil his work, or injure stock, or put some fellow wrangler into jeopardy.

"We'll, go on then!" Charlie said, and went and picked up his canteen and tossed it to Sefton only a little harder than necessary. Sefton caught it neatly.

These two hard-case youngsters, barely grown men, though each had worked at back-breaking droving for years, had each killed his man, had each bedded more turkey-whores and soddy's daughters than they could remember, still were growing into different men.

Sefton grew fiercer, harder, *denser* with each year. The wild boy who'd drawn—or, to be more accurate, had commenced to draw—on Ben Thompson, was becoming a man and fighter, grim and determined, of a kind that even Thompson would be careful of.

Not so for Potts. Charlie, like Sefton, two years older than Lee at twenty-four, had already seemed, as drovers often did, to have decided to stay a boy. A tough, dangerous, hard working boy, but never quite a man. Not for Charlie the responsibility of a place of his own someday. Not for Charlie any responsibility at all, but taking orders, and obeying them with a will. For Sid Sefton, Lee thought, anything might yet be possible.

Charlie would be this Charlie, forever.

Years before, Potts had made his mistake, gotten a Bit hand named Peach shot to death in a dishonorable way. Young Lee Morgan had done that killing, had been tricked into it.

Peach dead, Lee sent on the run and kept there, until Catherine Dowd's money and Boise lawyers had finally settled the matter. And sad Charlie, for one moment of drunken spite, ruined. He had never been able to forgive himself.

Lee stood before the fire in the gathering dusk seeing, high over the birch grove, the faint silver disk of the moon growing brighter. It would be full dark soon, and cool. He could smell the mountains in the evening breeze, a smell of cold stone mingling with the pine-breath and alder.

Potts . . . Sefton . . . Clevenger . . . Ford. Ford was fitting in fine . . . had all the makings. Tough, leaned-down little man, an owl-hooter at one time for sure. Had the mark of a second holster on the left side of his gun belt. Must have taken that left-hand gun off when he'd gone straight. Nervy, too, of strangers . . . Ford looked to do just fine, for a permanent hand on the Bit.

Lee heard the sizzle, and looked down as the little wrangler dumped sliced bacon from a strip of birch bark into the soot crusted iron spider that squatted in the fire. The coffee pot was already bubbling and snorting on the coals beside it, the rich smell of fresh-hammered beans rising up and over the odors of the coming night.

Couldn't be many better lives to lead than this.

"Now, say . . ." Ray, quietly, come up to stand beside him, looking over the camp. "How are you figurin' these people to come against us?"

Lee looked around him at the grove, packed with restless horses, already shadowy in the failing light, and out behind him, an expanse of rolling meadow. Clumps of scrub out there but no real cover, nothing to matter.

"What I'd do," he said, "were I them—I'd make a fuss out there, send some riders shooting off their revolvers, yelling. Then I'd come down through the woods on foot, just a few men, get into that grove while all the fuss was popping, cut the lines, and spook me a herd of horses."

Clevenger looked around, thinking about it.

"Well," he said finally, tugging at the ends of his mustachios with thick, calloused fingers, "well—I suppose those people might do somethin' of that sort were they to be up to anythin' at all!"

"Figure they will, Ray. Set out the men as you think best." Had to give the old man his due—Clevenger an old man at fifty-one, gray and worn, beaten down by years of endless work, muscle-tearing and bone-breaking, twelve hours a day, day in and day out, in all weathers. Let him set the men and see how well he does it, even disagreeing.

Lee had had to learn lessons fast in the difficult art of handling men, men almost always older and more experienced. Men as fierce as hawks, too, and dangerous if they considered themselves touched in their honor. It would be best, Lee thought, if Sid was left back of the herd, deep in the woods beyond, to cut at those rustlers come sneaking down. Sefton, and maybe the new man, Ford.

Potts, Clevenger, and Lee could handle the riders over that open field. Could handle them nicely, in moonlight.

Unless, of course, he was wrong, had misjudged Packwood, and the rest of the men who lived in the Roughs. Or, having judged them right, was wrong on how Packwood intended to go about his theft. Could damn certain be wrong about that, and look a fool to the men because of it.

And perhaps he was a fool, since he found he preferred an attack and a fight (and killing for sure) rather than nothing and him proved wrong. "Vanity of vanities—all is vanity." Lee, like most of the wranglers, avoided church when he could—that is, when Catherine Dowd didn't ask for his escort there, intending, Lee supposed, to see that he was set off to the people of Grover and the countryside as a more considerable citizen than a common ranch foreman and wrangler. Still, he did duck out when she let him. More doing at the Ace and the Union than in a dozen churches, brimstone sermons or not.

Clevenger sucked a tooth, and considered, taking his time. "Weeell . . . I suppose may as might put young Sid back up in them woods. Charley, too, I suppose . . . An' you an' me an' Ford'll stand along here, do any come shootin'."

Good enough, though a little sad, too. Ray hadn't

noticed quite how far Charlie Potts had slipped . . . hadn't quite made up his mind about Ford.

Still, good enough.

"Good enough, Ray. Set 'em out."

CHAPTER FOUR

At full dark, Sid and Charlie were already gone from the fire, strolled off in soft moonlight as if for a piss, and now hunkered under some tilted birch or beside some dwarf alder stump out back behind the horse grove, their rifles across their laps, their eyes and ears on the stretch.

Lee, Clevenger and Ford lingered at the fire, eating the last of the bacon and fried biscuit from birch bark slabs, licking grease from their fingers after each bite.

When they were finished, had scraped the fry-pan clean with the last pieces of biscuit, tramped the fire down to embers, passed Charlie Potts' canteen for a swallow each, filled their cracked enamel coffee cups and doused those last embers with the dregs—then it was sit back, or lean back on their saddles, and light up pipes (Clevenger and Ford) or a cigar stub (Lee) and contemplate the night.

The moon was now up nearly full, silvering the soft, feathery tops of the grove. The shifting wind, cooler and cooler, sometimes brought them the rich smell of the herd, the soft sounds of shifting horses.

"Them horses ain't restin'."

"I know it, Ray—they'll settle."

Lee was considering replacing his old Henry—a nice weapon, but carrying the poor short .44 cartridge. Might be best to get one of the Winchesters . . . Sid swore by his.

Lee puffed on the last of his cigar, feeling comfortable, feeling the long, narrow weight of the Henry across his lap. A handsome piece, though. Never be a better looking weapon. He had only four or five of the Grover House special cigars left . . . have to go easy on them, to last until San Francisco.

"Say," Ford said, a few feet off, leaning on his saddle in the moonlight, the hazy silver air dotted by the single bright crimson spot of the coals of his pipe as he drew on it. "Say, you know I heard in town Bob Fitzsimmons is champ?"

"Now, there's a lie," Clevenger said. "Someone sure is pullin' your ding-dong, Ford. That sailor-boy never saw the day he could beat the champ!"

"Done it, though," Ford said. "That's the word at the tonsorial."

"Shit."

"Champ couldn't come out to the bell."

"Believe that, you'd believe anythin'."

"That's the word."

"That that sissy barber tellin' that?"

"Nope. Fat one."

"Sounds the McCoy," Lee said. "Too bad."

"Great God almighty—Fitzsimmons!"

"Somebody was bound to take the belt," Ford said, and coughed and knocked the dottle out of his pipe into the palm of his other hand.

"Maybe so," Clevenger said. "But a sailor!"

They were silent awhile, thinking about that change in the world's affairs. Lee had seen the champion once, in Boise—a grinning man, Lee's height and build, with a quick blue eye and shock of red hair. Catnip to the ladies, supposedly. The champion had been standing, with friends and hangers-on, in the anteroom of the National Bank in Boise, talking and chattering like a dandy-sport, which of course he was. As Lee'd stood by the doorway, watching, the boxer had reached casually out, still talking—telling some yarn—and had caught a fly by the room's open window with an easy almost passing curving motion of his arm.

Now, lying before the extinguished fire, the warmth of its bed still pressing gently against his face, Lee recalled the last thing that Catherine Dowd had said to him. An odd thing for even an unusual woman to be saying . . . "A pistol draw with angles to it, can get no faster . . ." Something of that sort. Lee thought it might equally be some philosophical observation or indeed his dead father's expert observation. He remembered Corbett's motion in catching that fly . . . No elbows or angles to that.

A parabola, Lee supposed. Some mathematical curve. He smiled, thinking of writing to Corbett or going to see him in San Francisco to talk about the mathematicals of his strikes and punches. Doubtless some Eastern newspaper man had already exhausted the subject.

"Well . . . now, I'll be damned," Clevenger said, several feet away, dimly seen by moonlight, "if I don't have me a mouthful of crow."

Then Lee heard and felt at once the distant, soft, rolling mutter of hoofbeats.

Ford put his pipe away, stood up with his rifle in his hands, then walked away to the right without a word. Clevenger grunted with effort and climbed to his feet. "Keep your head down, boy." And stumped off to the left, toward a small tree trunk, its bark shining dark silver, fallen years before at the north edge of the grove.

Lee stood, the Henry feeling light as a walking stick in his hand, and listened, his head cocked to one side. Half a mile off, and coming fast—and wanting it *known* they were coming fast. Now was the time some people would be sneaking down the slopes to the back of the grove. And if Charlie or Sid had gone to sleep back there, liable to wake up just as their throats were cut. Lee had no notion of Packwood or any of the men of the Roughs being particular about killing.

The hoofbeats were louder. Six horses at least, maybe eight. Lee'd expected more, but likely Packwood, knowing his men, had held most of them off from trouble until he could bring them in in a bunch after this demonstration.

Far down the meadow, Lee saw the flash of revolver fire and, an instant later, the dull thuds of the reports. Taking no chances about drawing the camp's attention that way! Sid and Charlie better be wide awake back in those woods. *Wide* awake.

A bullet drifted humming by a few feet to Lee's right. Moonlight shooting . . .

He stepped two paces to his left, dropped to one knee, levered a round into the Henry's chamber, and sighted down the long, shining barrel to swift, shuttling movement over deep grass, galloping horses running in and out of moon shadows as they came down upon the camp—and suddenly, at a yell, swerved away to the left in a trample of hooves. Lee could hear leather creak as the riders leaned in their saddles at the turn. Saw clods of grass fly, looking frosted with evening dew. Revolver flashes—a swarm of bees buzzing high across the clearing.

He sighted on a horse's chest as they turned. Fired—his left eye held tight closed so as not to be blinded by the flash—and must have missed. A confusion of men out there. He didn't think Packwood had come in with them at all.

Then shots from the left and right. Ford and Clevenger firing time after time, like a squad of soldiers. Lee looked left and saw the bright orange flashes of Ford's rifle. Each flash to the right of the one before; the little man was moving after every shot.

Lee brought his head slightly across the stock of the Henry to sight with his left eye—lined down on a man riding out there bolt upright in the moonlight. His right eye held closed this time, Lee held the sight on this fellow as he galloped away at an angle, and shot at him.

For the time it took to take a breath, the horseman sat as straight in the saddle as a general, still riding away. Then he suddenly hunched over, as if the Henry's bullet had loitered on its way to strike him, threw up a hand and rolled out of the saddle limp as wet linen. Staring, one-eyed Lee saw him hit the grass, bounce up, and collapse into the silver green again.

A hurt man, or dead. The Henry had jolted against Lee's shoulder in that particular, solid way that weapons had when there was a hit for sure.

Gunfire behind him.

Revolver fire.

Lee turned to stare back over the corralled horse herd to a quick blaze of shooting along the line of the woods. Men yelling.

He dropped the Henry and got up and ran toward the grove, the Bisley Colt's already in his hand. Darker in here—the moonlight dappled by the trees. Behind him as he ran, Lee heard Clevenger shout something and laugh. Rifle fire. They should be able to hold those horsemen. They should certainly be able to hold.

The revolver shooting rippled brightly in front of him again. Crashes of sound. A horse was screaming. Some damn fool had shot a horse.

"Hey, now!" A man calling to him came walking out of the trees.

"*Sid?*"

"Hell no, you son of a bitch!" The man raised a dull-metaled pistol and aimed at Lee as if he were shooting at bottles on a bet. He had no hat on, shaggy hair and a beard.

Lee shot him through the middle and the man sat down suddenly at the report as if the noise had knocked him down. Lee ran past him, not more than a few feet away, but the man sat silent, staring at him, making no effort to raise his pistol again.

Lee ran as hard as he could wishing to God he was barefoot, didn't have the damn heavy boots weighing at him as he ran—angled off past the lariats, the heaving, neighing horses, and saw Sid Sefton, cool as a chunk of marble, back out into the moonlight from a patch of brush shooting left and right at some person back in that tangle.

Lee called to him and Sid glanced over his shoulder. He looked pleased. Another shot was fired from the woods at him, and he frowned and fired back with both revolvers, almost together. The man in the woods fired again, and Lee was certain Sefton would be hit, standing out there so plain. "*Get down!*" And saw Sid turn toward him again, sticking out his tongue at him like a kid.

"No need . . . !" Sefton called as Lee ran past him, ducking another shot. Lee fired directly at that muzzle blast and drove on into the scrub—worried, for some reason, more about getting a branch tip stuck into his eye than being shot.

He crashed into brush, stumbled and slipped to one knee.

A gun went off in his face. He felt the quick sparking sting of powder. There was an odd moment of silence, as if the man who'd fired at him was embarrassed, as if he'd done something like farting in front of people . . . women.

Lee knew where the man was; there was a place almost in front of him that was too dark. He fired into it three times and in the flash of the first shot, saw a boy staring out at him, mouth stretched in a grimace of fear. Light colored hair like cornsilk. At the second shot, which came so fast after the first, Lee saw that he'd hit the boy and was killing him. Lee tried to stop the third shot, then, but it was too late. As if it had an impatient life of its own, as if it were tired of not being put to proper use, the Colt's bucked in his hand, the flare of light exposed the boy, no more than twelve years old, twelve or thirteen, falling back in a spray of blood black as theatre velvet in the moonlight.

Lee thought he would regret doing that, and considered that he had only one more round in the Colt's while he turned left and bucked hard through the brush, back along the split rails they'd used to close the wood side of the grove.

"*Potts!*"

Sefton all right, but Potts perhaps not. Shouldn't have been back here.

"*Potts!*" A shot came cracking at Lee, and he ducked long after the bullet twanged away. Now, where was that drunk son of a bitch?

Lee heard a man running, up higher in the woods —thought of saving his shot, but then thought not and threw the round up there with a *bang!* and flash of light. "*Jeesus!*" a man screamed. Lee didn't know if he'd hit him or scared him. Scared him, most likely.

He heard Charlie Potts talking. " . . . Now there's something."

"Charlie?"

"Right here. Hell, I'm right here! No need for all that carryin' on!" After he stopped talking, Lee saw him sitting behind a narrow tree-trunk, his revolver on his lap, reloading.

"Are you hit?"

"Not hit an' haven't done none, either. These damn birds got no guts for a fight at all!"

The night had become so quiet, Lee realized he and Potts were speaking in whispers. No more gunshots. The horses were still making noise. Not the screaming one, though. That animal was quiet; must have died.

"It's all over," Potts said, speaking up. "That wasn't much, either."

Lee remembered the young boy's face as he'd fired into him.

"You get you one?" Potts finished with his revolver, stood up and put it away.

"Yes."

"Not surprised, way you was runnin' around blazin' away like Wild Bill Hickok!" Potts turned to the tree trunk, unbuttoned his trouser flies, and began to pee. "Never saw anybody like a fight so much as you, Lee . . . damn if I ever did."

"*Say, Leeee . . . !*" Clevenger.

Lee shouted back. "Over here! And look out, there's one down in the grass with a pistol—hurt!"

"Keep an eye out, Charlie," Lee said, turning to go, "one of them might have lingered."

Potts, still peeing, laughed. "Lingered, my ass. Those boys are halfway to Canada by now."

"You keep an eye out just the same . . ."

As he skirted the north end of the grove and walked toward the fire pit, Lee saw two men standing, looking at something in the grass. Clevenger and Ford. By God, he hadn't lost a man! There was a sound, though, somebody crying. As he walked closer, Lee heard it coming from where Clevenger and Ford were standing. He came up and saw a man lying on his side in the moonlight. A man with a beard. It was the fellow he'd shot.

"Are you all right?"

"I didn't get touched, Ray."

"Damn poor shootin' those people were doin'." Clevenger puffed out his cheeks and blew like a tired horse. His mustache, the Burnsides under his Stetson brim, were snow white in the pale light. "This poor creature sure got touched."

The man lying in the grass was crying like a heart-broken child. He lay on his side, his hands clutched to his belly, his legs, knees bent, drawn up hard to ease the pain.

Clevenger leaned over him. "Say, Mister, you're not doin' any good with all that bawlin'."

The man seemed to hear him, opened his eyes and took a deep, shuddering breath. "Martha . . ." he said.

Lee didn't know whether the fellow was talking to them or to his absent woman.

"What say, Mister Morgan?" Ford said, the little man standing still, his wrinkled jockey's face shadowed by his hat.

It was not a real question.

Lee held out his hand, and Ford, with no hesitation, drew his revolver and handed it over. It was a big Smith & Wesson Russian Model .44.

Lee cocked it, stepped forward and leaned down over the weeping man, and shot him through the head. The man's skull cracked with a strange smacking sound as the bullet went through.

That shot was the loudest shot of all.

It had taken time to settle the horses, more time to go out and look for shot men. They never found a man Clevenger claimed to have shot out in the grass. And they didn't find the man Lee had shot out there, either. They found a dead horse but nothing else except a man's hat.

They found the dead boy in the brush, though. No older than twelve or thirteen, for sure. "That little bandit must have shot at me half a dozen times," Sefton said, "and not hit once. Nor I him. But I did hit a man up in the trees. I hit him hard."

As he must have, there being a tree—a silver birch—wet with dark blood all down one side, right where Sid claimed to have shot. But if the man had died, he'd crawled away to do it.

"Lord almighty," Clevenger said, seeing the dead boy. "What fool gave this snot-nose two pistols and the leave to come up here?" The boy had had two Remington revolvers, converted from cap-and-ball some time ago, it looked like. Clevenger bent over the boy, who looked small and like a thrown away thing there in the scrub, and set his finger tip to the three holes, black and soaked in blood, as distinct in the moonlight as they might be in the light of an afternoon. The moon was setting now, throwing shine deep under the trees. Clevenger measured the spacing of the wounds with his finger, like a man proud of his shooting a running deer. Not one of the bullet holes was more than a finger from another.

“Now that,” Clevenger said, “is a high quality of revolver shooting.”

“Especially on such a small target,” Lee said, surprising himself. They were all standing, looking down at the kid.

Clevenger looked up at him, startled. “You’d rather be lyin’ here, ’stead of him?”

“No,” Lee said.

“I guess not.” Clevenger got to his feet with a grunt. “Charlie, you get that shovel off the horse-pack. We got two to put under.” He dusted his hands and turned to Lee, his face harsh-carved by moon-shadows. “What now, boy?” as Potts walked away to get the shovel.

“They’ll come for real at dawn,” Lee said and no longer doubted it. “They won’t ride down.” He nodded up into the woods. “They’ll come walking down from there, like soldiers—try and lay down more lead than we can stand. Make us ride out or kill us.”

Clevenger didn’t seem to doubt it; neither did Ford or Sefton.

“An’ we meet ’em back of the grove?”

“No, Ray.” It came to Lee as he spoke. “We’ll get set up here at this end of the rise, up high in the woods and wait for them to get past us, get them down-slope . . .”

“Back-shoot the sons-of-bitches,” Sefton said.

Lee nodded, then was not sure that Sid had seen the nod in this uncertain light. “That’s right,” he said. “Every single one we can.”

“Better leave somebody down here,” Clevenger said, “else they could just run on down to the horses, cut 'em loose, spook 'em an' keep on goin'."

He was right.

"Sid . . ."

"Hell, no!" Clevenger said. "I ain't runnin' around up in that tangle. You leave it to me and Ford. We'll nest in real good down here an' dish 'em some hot hell, do they make it this far!"

"All right," Lee said. "But get you good cover—there'll be a bunch, and this time there'll be a man leading them."

They could hear Potts coming back with the shovel.

"Never fear, boy," Clevenger said. "Take more'n an asshole to scare an old shit like me!"

Lee slept, and in his sleep was once more a young boy on the Rifle River, high above Cree. He was riding a pony named Buddy through the meadow just below the house. His mother had called him, and he was pretending not to hear . . . didn't want to come in to supper . . . .

The evening light was falling like lace curtains across the deep valley beyond; as the sun drifted down behind the western peaks a great shadow came creeping like a flood of dark water over the valley's green, filling the bowl of forest and pasture like that dark water he had found in deep woods, in small pools of rain and drainage water puddled there amid the leaves in autumn.

She was calling him.

He looked up and saw his mother standing at the cabin door, smiling. Even at the distance, Lee was certain of her smile. She had her apron on over her long blue dress. She lifted a hand to him, and he heard her call again, then saw her turn her head to talk to someone inside. Buddy was drifting down the hillside, cropping at the long grass. Drifting on down, no matter how Lee sawed the reins . . . .

Now, Lee was sorry he'd been so smart. Sorry he had not gone right in. It was harder to see her; he had to twist his neck hard to see her in the doorway. And as he did that, he saw a man come out of the cabin to stand beside her. Put his arm around Lee's mother's waist as if that were the most natural thing in the world to do.

The man was young, his hair dark, so it was an instant before Lee saw that it was his father, come home.

He woke with a jolt and gasp that sounded in his ears as loud as a shout, wedged in, his neck uncomfortable against the huge rough round curve of a fallen tree.

The moon was down, and had long been down. The night, quite cold, had that absolute and fragile darkness that stood just before the coming of light. Pine scent, horse smell from the saddle blanket he was wrapped in. No sounds on this ridge of woods and berry scrub except for slight shifts of leaves at some dawn breeze, a drowsy bird calling far across the wooded slope.

"You awake, Lee?" A soft mutter to his left. Charlie Potts—and sited too close to him. Charlie must have moved in, wanted some company. Lee didn't answer, lay trying to recapture that last vision of his mother . . . of both of them there on Rifle River.

"You awake?"

"Be still, Charlie, and move on back to where you were."

"I will—I will. I was wonderin', Lee—will we have some time to spend in Frisco? Say a week?"

"I suppose. Now . . ."

"I will—I will. Well, I wondered—it's said to be hell on earth for a spree, that city."

"So it's said. Now, get on back to where you were!"

"All right. All right . . ." The faintest breath of whiskey on the odors of the woods.

It came to Lee that Charlie Potts was scared stiff, had certainly retrieved his canteen and drunk from it.

Lee raised his voice a little, taking that chance. "Charlie!"

A silence. Then, "What . . . ?"

"Don't you shoot all these fice-dogs. You leave some for me and Sid!"

"Hell—I'll leave you the mangy ones." Sounds of him settling in, pushing a branch aside. Further off, but not as far off as Lee had placed him first.

Charlie Potts. Lee saw now, as if this darkness gave the right sort of light for it, that he had done very badly by Charlie Potts. When the business had been settled—the killing of George Peach, the wounding of that deputy, Chook—then had been the time to have settled with Charlie for causing the fuss. Lee saw now that he had done the worst possible thing by forgiving Charlie, by seeming to forget it, by letting it pass.

So he had left the corruption in the wound.

It was clear now what he should have done. Should have called Charlie out years before. Taken him out beyond the stables and fought him—beaten him to a frazzle any way he could in payment for that piece of mischief-making. Then it would have been up to Charlie to clear off the place or take his whipping and stay.

That was the thing to have done, and Lee hadn't done it. He'd liked Charlie, pitied him, and let it ride.

Well, it was riding Charlie near to death.

Occurred to Lee that perhaps it was not too late even now to lance that wound, to drain the corruption out of it.

Perhaps not too late, even after these years.

Lee thought he saw the outlines of the trees around him. He slipped the saddle blanket from his shoulders and sat up, turning to face across the slope of hill. The receiver of the Henry was ice cold beneath his wrist. Yes . . . outlines of the trees. The bigger branches were now a little darker than the sky beyond them.

Daylight coming on steady.

Lee heard Charlie stirring off to the right. Hadn't gone to sleep, at least. Listened for Sefton; heard no sound at all. Sid had chosen a stand further upslope, almost to the crest of the low ridge leading down to the hasty corral, the horses. If Packwood . . . if the rustlers did come this way, heading downslope to the herd, they would, many of them, be dead meat under the fire of three repeating rifles above and to one side.

Lee couldn't think of anything he had forgotten, had neglected to do. He musn't lose a man because of something he had not done. No excuse for that. No excuse for throwing a man's life away by mistake.

Damn bunch of horses. Goddamn senseless things . . . .

He hitched up higher on one knee. Now he could see clear down the slope. It looked like some Indian silver work Catherine Dowd had on a fine end table at the house. Black trees in silver light. And growing lighter, all the time.

Lee slowly, carefully worked the Henry's lever action, hearing the "click an' clack" louder than it ever seemed.

Sid Sefton's Winchester sounded a soft echo, higher up, to the left. Lee hoped to God that Charlie had not drunk enough to put himself to sleep. They might do this thing with three rifles. They sure as hell wouldn't do it with less.

Plenty of ammunition, at any rate. Boxes of the stuff jamming their coat pockets. Lee's buckskin jacket was chill with the morning's damp. Lighter now. Getting lighter every minute. Might have been better, after all, to have stampeded a few of the geldings off. Let those white trash go chasing them . . . might have been cheaper . . . might have been a wiser thing to do.

Lee thought that he might be afraid, and found that he wasn't. *Too damn stupid*, he supposed. *Think you can whip and shoot your way out of anything.* A stray bullet in his guts would teach him different. That was for sure. That fellow last night, with the beard, likely thought he would live forever, too.

Had he forgotten anything? Might the people from the Roughs come riding after all? Find the herd below unprotected with just Ray and Ford down there and on the wrong side of the grove, at that . . .

Better pray that Packwood was not that smart, to double and double his thinking in that fashion.

Just pray.

Dawn was here, and the forest and its hillside were plain to see. Lee pulled a box of ammunition from his jacket pocket, set it on the broad top of the log to be within reach, but not so close he'd knock it down into the brush to be lost while he was firing.

He could see clearly anything he chose to look at. No sunlight yet, but a fine even white dawn light. No motion, though. No one moving.

Could be wrong. Could be they weren't coming this way at all . . . Lee strained his ears for the sounds of hoofbeats down on the level.

Silence. Except for birds. All of them waking up now. Making noise out of every tree, it sounded like. Would be a pretty morning, except for this fighting.

Lee pushed a little against the weight of the log before him to see if it would give . . . if it was set solidly, or might roll away suddenly in the fight and leave him defenceless, as good as naked to the bullets.

Scared a little, after all. The log was solid as stone.

Pretty soon, it would be too light, too late in the morning, for them to be coming like soldiers. Not the kind of people who would stand in broad daylight to be shot at, not like your regular infantry soldiers. Not that bunch.

Lee could hear himself breathe, it was so quiet.

So quiet.

No birds singing.

He slid the Henry's barrel up across the log and, as if they had waited for that, like a sign, two men came walking down through the woods.

Lee saw Packwood's hand at once. The men were barefoot. Might have been in their stockings, if they'd had them. But not boots. So simply, Packwood had them quieter than they would have been.

These two looked like brothers and, except for their careful tender-footed way of walking through the viney tangle, didn't seem to be fearful of shooting.

They walked down the first, steepest slope of the ridge side by side. Both men unshaven with drooping dark mustaches. Both thin as bird-pecked skeletons. They were just under two hundred yards away from him, Lee thought. The near man was carrying a Spencer rifle. The other man—his brother—looked to have a shotgun of some sort over his arm. Both man carried pistols.

So easy were they, so casually walking, that Lee had a momentary notion that they might be men out hunting, and not rustlers or Packwood's people at all.

Then another man came over the ridge and down. He was a fat fellow, barefoot also, with what looked to be a new Winchester rifle in his hands. He had a knife at his belt but no pistol.

Three more men came down after him. One man, who looked to have most of his teeth missing, Lee didn't know. The other two men were the Bergenreich brothers.

Lee saw a bunch coming down into the woods further on; he couldn't make out any that he knew, though. They were a ways off. With that bunch, it made ten or twelve men.

Considerable odds.

Getting lighter now. There was a warmth to the light along the ridge. The sun was rising. Lee wondered why Packwood had left it so late. May have been fearful these people would just skulk off if he couldn't see them and the shooting got fierce.

A man in overalls, with no rifle but carrying two pistols ready in his hands, came down into the woods next. He had shoes on his feet—must have refused Packwood's orders about that. All the men were getting well down the slope. Soon they'd be too damn far down the slope for good shooting.

Lee saw Packwood (wearing *his* boots) come strolling over the rise a good ways down. He looked smaller than Lee recalled him, but he was wearing the Mexican hat.

One of the men below had turned to look back the way they'd come, and Lee saw Packwood step down past a big pine and motion to the men to keep going. They were, some of them, a fair way down the slope already.

Lee took a good rest across the log, got a fine bead on one of the two men who'd come into the woods first—it was the one carrying the Spencer rifle—and shot him.

It was a distance shot, nearly three-hundred yards, and the sound still rang in Lee's ears when Sid, to his left, and Potts, to the right and closer, both fired at once.

Lee had hit his man. He stared down the Henry's barrel as the fellow put out an arm to lean against a birch tree. Then, as if too tired for that effort, fell down.

The other men moved, scattered away through the woods or fell where they were (one or two of them maybe hit by Sid and Charlie). Most began to fire back and the air around Lee was filled with humming, snapping noises. He kept his head up, though, trying to find Packwood—sorry now he hadn't fired at him first, however near out of range the others had been.

The man in the Mexican hat was gone, ducked out of sight and shooting back for sure.

A bullet whacked into the log in front of Lee; he felt the jar in his arms, and ducked down despite himself. Then, behind the log, Lee heard a fast series of gunshots ringing far down the slope—Clevenger and Ford taking a hand. Should pull the spine out of this trash, being shot at front and back . . .

He sat up again, the Henry across the log, looking for a target. The woods were growing brighter by the moment, the leaves at the treetops edged with sunlight. A light haze of gunpowder drifted through the woods.

The log jolted again. A piece of bark three feet down from Lee suddenly tore half free and stood out like a rooster's comb. Lee looked hard down-slope—saw nothing at first, then, he was pretty sure, a man's leg stretched out from under a patch of berry brush, where he was hiding. A man's leg for sure. Barefoot.

Lee leaned up over the bulk of the log, heard the

flat *whack whack!* of rounds being fired at him, drew a fine bead and hit that fellow's leg as sure as shooting.

Someone was screaming; Lee didn't know who. The firing down by the horses was very fierce. Revolver shooting now as well as rifle fire. An occasional booming report . . . a shotgun, likely. Clevenger and Ford were catching hell, no doubt. Dishing it out as well.

Potts shouted something; Lee couldn't make out what he was yelling but saw, about a stone's throw down the slope, two men come breaking out of the scrub, running. They were coming right up toward him; Lee could see their bare feet as they ran, hear the crashing brush as they came. Their faces were contorted with effort and fear. Lee didn't know one of them, a squat old man in homespun; the other was one of the Bergenreiches. Both men had revolvers in their hands, and as they saw Lee, they began to fire at him as they ran.

It surprised Lee and, for a moment, scared him. It was the damndest thing to see—those furious faces. Firing at him, running at him like madmen. He didn't know what in hell they thought they were doing!

"Shoot! *Shoot!*"

Sid Sefton was out of the trees above him and to the left, firing his Winchester at the men, shouting at Lee. Lee saw that it would take too much time to fool with levering and sighting the rifle. He could hear them gasping with effort as they ran.

Lee let the Henry fall, stood to clear his draw, fired the Bisley Colt's, and knocked Klaus Bergenreich down with the bullet. Bergenreich, big as a bear, rolled in the brush and heaved himself up again as the stocky man, old and white haired, was hit by one of Sefton's rifle slugs in his groin and staggered sideways down the slope, dropping his pistol and clutching at himself with both hands already red as paint.

Lee fired at Bergenreich again and might have missed him, because Bergenreich got back up onto his feet. Lee fired a third time, and saw the big man's shirt flirt out where the bullet struck him, just under his left arm as he was turning, still holding his revolver.

This last was a killing shot, and Bergenreich squatted down suddenly, his mouth opening and shutting like trout drowning in air. Then he fell over onto his side, his head downhill. Lee saw a dark stain spreading over the seat of the man's trousers.

"*You O.K.?*" Sid, standing up-slope, the Winchester lowered. Bullets came buzzing across the slope like lazy bees.

"Hell, yes! You get *your* ass down!" His fault, to be daydreaming and let those two fools get that close. Sid had likely saved his bacon. When Lee glanced up again, he saw that Sefton had ducked back into the trees.

But why the hell had those men come up that way?

Lee got his answer in a crash of gunfire down below. Clevenger and Ford . . . He'd set up his trap too damn well! These fool rustlers thought they were dead-falled, trapped front and back, and they were panicking like stampeding cattle!

Lee heard a man shouting down in the woods. Then the brush seemed to erupt with men all along the slope, a dozen men at least, rushing, stumbling, leaping back up the hillside, shooting as they came.

Drive them away—drive them sideways across the slope! Then let 'em over the ridge! Lee thought he was shouting that to Sid and Charlie, but he wasn't sure. He'd reloaded the Colt's faster than he'd ever done it, holstered it, and was firing the Henry as fast as he could lever it—not so much trying to hit, as trying to force that rushing terror-stricken bunch away by sheer volume of gun blasts, the smashing weight of bullet strikes.

Out of the corner of his eye Lee saw Charlie Potts for the first time since the shooting had started . . . *thirty seconds ago? A minute?* Potts had come out into the open, was kneeling on one knee firing into the mob with his revolver as they scrambled up the slope, yelling, shouting out curses, shooting wildly back at Lee and the two wranglers.

Charlie was firing at these fear maddened men as calmly, as deliberately as if they were bottles propped along a fence, and must be hitting, though in that wild charge, men slipped and fell and then got up to climb again shot or not.

Bad luck, Lee thought, and let the empty Henry fall to draw the Colt's. Bad luck. And my mistake. I should have left them a way out.

Seven or eight men were still standing from the rush—*and where the hell is Packwood?*—and they came up to Lee, shooting.

Lee came out from behind the fallen log, fired into a fat man's chest—it was the man he'd seen before—

and scrambled sideways as two of the others shot at him. A round went singing past him and smacked into a tree like a blow from a baseball bat. *The next one into my back.* Lee turned again, uphill, dodging and jinking like a hunted rabbit, and heard the "*bang . . . bang . . . BANG!*" A man shouting.

It seemed a miracle he hadn't been hit. Lee fell full out into the brush, then twisted around to see a man stopping not fifteen feet away, staring at him, chest heaving, some sort of small blued steel revolver in his hand. Lee had never seen the man before. Lee lifted the Bisley, leveled it, and while the man still seemed to be getting his breath, shot him through the belly.

The man who looked like some drover down on his luck, sandy hair like a Scotchman, appeared then to throw his small revolver away, try to walk away after it, tangled his feet in something, and fell, small branches crackling, into a bush.

Two more came kicking through the scrub, and one fired well over Lee's head. This man had a big nose, and eyes as white as water. His trousers were patched to a fare-thee-well. Lee shot him once, high in the chest, and when he reeled from that blow and fell into his friend, Lee killed that man, firing a round through his head, the bullet dotting the man's cheek with a sudden inky black dot, then kicking out a wad of brains on the other side, that stuck against a tree.

The man with the big nose sank down into the brush with his dead friend, and looked at Lee as if they had trouble in common.

I'm a dead man, Lee thought. One round left in

the Colt's. He rolled over, his jacket catching in a tendril of briar, and climbed to his feet, feeling worn out, too tired to take another breath. He couldn't hear anything except a hard ringing in his ears from the gunshots.

Deaf as a post, he thought. And considered if, after all, he had a chance to reload. The man with the big nose had closed his eyes, and lay a few feet away from Lee, resting comfortably, it appeared, against the shoulder of his friend. Big Nose was still alive, though; Lee could see his chest moving.

A man came walking slowly between two trees, looked up and saw Lee. This man had an old black broadcloth suit on; his bare feet looked odd beneath the trousers. He had a rifle carried in one hand. A broad brown beard down across his chest. Brown eyes.

"Isn't this a hell of a thing?" he said to Lee.

When Lee didn't answer, the bearded man shook his head and walked on, grunting with the effort as he climbed up a little overgrown slant, where spring rains had washed some earth away beneath a rotted stump.

Lee watched him go, and didn't fire after him. He could still hear shooting even through the ringing in his ears, and concluded his ears were getting better. There was no one near him now except for the big nosed man with patched pants and he was resting quietly against his friend.

Lee began to think he would live, after all—and as if that had been an evil thought to be punished, two men came running through the trees. One of them was the man he'd seen who'd kept his shoes on.

They saw Lee, and turned together and shot at him to kill him.

A bullet snapped through the buckskin, shirt, and flesh just above Lee's gunbelt, at his left side. It made a popping sound as it went through. Other bullets, one or two, passed him by, twanging away as if they had business elsewhere and Lee, feeling somehow better for being hurt at last, took a cool and careful aim at that man who'd kept his shoes, certain that that was the one that had hit him, and with his last bullet, shot him plumb center—and that at a distance of fifty or sixty feet.

The man with shoes, who had a grim and savage face, unshaven and wrinkled as a snarling dog's, suddenly lost all his force and sank away, his revolver fallen, playing with rapid fingers at the middle of his chest, as if to indicate the trouble was there, to some magical physician hovering in the air.

The man with him fired back at Lee and missed. Lee didn't hear the bullet going past. He saw this fellow cock his piece to try again, try again, sighting carefully—and Charlie Potts stepped out beside Lee, took aim with his revolver, and shot the man down.

Put another into him as he thrashed.

Then he turned to Lee and said something, but Lee couldn't make out what it was, so Charlie raised his voice.

"Are we even now, God damn you?"

Lee answered, and heard his own voice oddly through the fading ringing in his ears.

"Even," he said. "Charlie, we're even all the way."

* * *

The woods were silent, full of streaming golden light as the sun rose. Eddies of gunpowder stank in their nostrils as Lee, Sefton, and Charlie Potts walked down through the vine tangles and berry bushes, through clearings bright with leafy light. Lee's side was hurting him badly, his left trouser leg was wet with blood, but the bleeding seemed to have slowed to a stop after Sid foleded a neckerchief over the neat in-and-out bullet hole through skin and meat just over Lee's hip bone.

"Not near deep enough to touch your guts," Sefton had said. "Looks like it's bled out clean."

"Shit," Potts had said, looking at it, "I seen skeeter bites bleed worse 'n that!" Charlie looked tired and happy, very pleased with himself.

When Sefton had fitted Lee's gunbelt up higher, to hold the neckerchief in place on the wound, the three of them set off down the slope, ignoring as if they could not hear him, a man crying out for help—the man with the big nose, Lee thought—in the woods above them.

They passed another wounded man on the way down through the trees, and for a moment Lee thought it might be Packwood, but it wasn't. It was a bulky, dark-complectioned man, lying up against a tree. His left leg was broken—by a fall or by a bullet—and he seemed to expect nothing from the three wranglers, but only sat watching them go by.

An exhilaration was seizing Lee and the others at what they'd been through, what they'd done.

"By God, this is the fight to out-match Adobe Walls!" Sid said. "You see what the hell we did here? Got to have put near ten men down—maybe more!" He did a shuffling dance on the mat of pine straw they were crossing, getting ready to climb down a steeper place. Sid danced a buck and wing a step or two there, shaking his Winchester like an Indian buck.

I'm alive, Lee thought, and likely don't deserve to be.

"I'm to blame for making those fellows fight us so hard," he said. "It was a sad trick to pen them up so they had to come at us. All we needed was to run them off."

Sefton and Charlie exchanged a quick glance as they walked on either side of him. "Shit, Lee—if we'd let 'em *off,* they'd of just come on back at us again!"

"Damn right," Sefton said. "Man—do you know what kind of fight this was? We're goin' to be famous in all the newspapers, I can tell you that!"

The three of them smelled rank with sweat and gunpowder as they climbed down through the trees. The smell—his own smell—bothered Lee. He wished they were a day closer to Calf Springs; the pleasure of washing in clear, cold water seemed to him at this moment the finest thing of all.

Lee saw the horse herd below, still corralled into the grove, Roy and Ford taking no chances. Charlie led out this last stretch, trotting, sliding down the year old bed of leaves to the flats below. Lee followed slower, favoring his side. The wound was likely nothing much, but it hurt something fierce, as if he were being injured there by a knife thrust cutting into him with every step. Not about to go jumping around like that fool, Potts . . . Sefton stayed back with him, talking about what a fight it had been.

Once out of the woods, walking on the flat around the west end of the birch grove, Lee felt something better. For a while there, climbing down through the trees, he thought the pain in his side was going to make him sick to his stomach. Or *something* was going to make him sick to his stomach. Have to do something about that big-nose man, fat fellow with the broken leg . . . have to make up his mind about that.

On the camp side of the grove, once clear of the corralled herd, Lee saw Charlie Potts standing by the fire pit, waiting for them. Three men were sitting with him, two of them with their hands in the air.

There was a man's body lying stretched out before the fire's dead gray bank of ashes, saddle blanket over the face. Lee saw the dead man's boots and trousers and, forgetting the injury to his side as if that wound belonged to another person entirely, started to run.

All the men standing there stared at him as he came to a stop, panting as if he'd run a mile instead of a hundred feet. Lee knelt down and pulled the horse blanket off Ray Clevenger's face as if the thick, dirty wool were smothering the old man. He did that, and then was sorry he'd done it.

All Ray's dignity was gone. The morning sunlight, bright as the limelight of a variety theatre, glowed upon a pinched old face, wrinkled and collapsed, white as paper. The big mustache appeared stuck on, like a pretender's at a party. One of Ray's eyes was almost closed, showing only a narrow crescent of bone white beneath the lid. The other eye, his right eye, was wide open, the pupil rolled up almost out of sight, the eyeball like a boiled egg in Clevenger's face.

More to have a reason to stop looking at the old man's face than anything else, Lee looked for Clevenger's wound. The dirty checked shirt had a tear well below the left pocket. There was blood there, but only a little.

"Did it hurt him much?" Lee said.

Ford, standing by the fire pit, aiming his revolver casually at the two men with their hands raised, said, "It hurt him like hell for a little bit." Said it without looking down from the men he covered.

Lee put the horse blanket back up where it had been.

"A rifle round took him there just while all the shootin' was lettin' up," Ford said. "Then these two came a-scootin' out of the woods. When I throwed down on 'em, they didn't show no fight."

"We surrendered to be taken to the law," Packwood said, as calm as he had been while Lee beat Phil Surtees. The heavy man stood almost easy, with his thick arms raised high. He'd lost his Mexican hat somewhere in the fight and, Lee thought, had been cool enough to figure that busting out downhill was the most likely way to get clear off when the shooting had started up behind him. Let the other fools try going back the way they'd come.

And would have made it and home free, but for Ford.

The man standing, hands high, beside Packwood, was a different article—lean and buck-toothed, scared as the jackrabbit he looked, clothes more rags than shirt and trousers. He wasn't saying anything.

"You hand us over to the law," Packwood said, "and we'll let a court judge the right of this fight, of you and your hired gunmen shooting at honest small ranchers come for payment of your tracking across their land." He said this as calm as a summer lake, his dark eyes as still and unworried as that lake's water. Having to hold his hands in the air didn't appear to discomfit him.

"How'd you like for me to cut you a new asshole?" Charlie Potts said to him. "I'd bet you're the damn skunk that killed Ray!"

Lee would have bet so, too.

"This land," he said to Packwood, from where he still knelt beside Clevenger's body, "is owned by Matthew Dowd Associates, out of Canada."

"So you say," Packwood said. He pursed his lips, thinking. "And I say that makes it worse—that you and these hoodlums are shooting at American citizens standing up for their rights against a parcel of British land-robbers."

"You're quite a talker, Sitting Bull," Sefton said. And a slow flush spread over Packwood's face. "I never," Sefton said, "saw an honest red nigger with such a combination of yellow streak and big mouth. Your white half must have been some trashy!"

Packwood, keeping his arms raised under the muzzle of Ford's revolver, nevertheless turned his head and gave Sid Sefton a terrible look, a sort of sudden gaping grin of rage. An animal's look. His eyes were bad to see.

Sid took just a half step back. "Well, God damn you then, come on!" He glanced at Ford. "Take that pistol off him, Ford! Give the fat mother-fucker his guns."

Lee got to his feet, his side giving him fits. "Settle down, now, Sid."

"Like hell!"

"I said settle down."

"Shit," Sid said. "Anybody can see this thing needs killin'."

"Yes," Lee said, as Packwood looked into his eyes, "Yes, he does." Packwood, he saw, was quite right—he and the others would have a fair enough argument, could they take it to Boise and the Territorial Court. An Idaho jury would likely be sympathetic to men they saw as small-holders fighting for land rights against a big Canadian company, against big ranchers . . . rich ranchers, as they would see it.

And Packwood was right again, that the rustling charge could not be proved: the men of the Roughs had, after all, not been *able* to rustle any stock. Might very well be presented as coming to demand their due in crossing tax over land they claimed as their own.

Lee found this Packwood too damn clever—the morning sun too bright. Ray Clevenger too damn dead. How in the world was he to do without the old man? Bud Bent, who might have taken Ray's place, was back at the ranch with Catherine Dowd. Potts and Sefton, both fine hands . . . but neither *old* enough. Not old enough to supply the horse sense Ray had.

Lee's side was hurting him bad.

Now, this clever Packwood—too clever to be let loose, even if Sid and Charlie . . . even if Ray's dead body would allow it.

Clever. Too damn clever.

Lee had a sudden vision of himself, the others, Catherine Dowd in a territorial court in Boise. Fumed oak panels . . . walnut benches. Judge Horace Jones, or Willoughby, or one of those high judges. And a jury of clerks and feed store owners.

And Packwood, playing a little fellow just trying to get along in a world of robber barons.

It wouldn't do.

"Charlie," Lee said, "go pick up his *buscardero* belt."

"His guns?"

"That's right." Lee looked at Packwood, and the dark man's thick, square hands. Powerful, quick hands.

"Put your hands down, Packwood—ease yourself."

Packwood pursed his lips, glanced at Ford and Ford's revolver, then put his hands down. The other man kept his hands up.

"Charlie, I told you to do something."

"Well—hell." Charlie looked at Ford, as if expecting him to say something.

"They're over there by that busted birch," Ford said, "In the grass."

"If you're expecting me to fight with you, Morgan . . ."

"I believe you will."

Charlie went stomping off.

"Why in the world take any chance with this asshole?" Sid said. "Hell—I'll kill him now the same as I would any bug that came crawling!"

"Mister Mathews," Packwood said, "take notice. These men intend to murder me."

"Murder you, you son-of-a-bitch!" Sid said. "You got Ray killed an' you got a bunch of your own killed up there, too!"

"I could hang you, if you prefer that to a fight," Lee said.

"Watch now, Mister Mathews—murder," Packwood said. He did not seem frightened. Only deliberate. It occured to Lee that Packwood was more than a little mad. That calmness . . . like a bulky animal, rather than a man.

Mathews, the rabbity man, still stood with his hands high, and appeared to wish he were a long way from the spot. He had nothing to say.

The sun was so bright, it had a glare to it even this early in the morning. Lee could smell, faintly, the odor of burnt wood still rising from the fire pit. The birds, silent during all the shooting, shouts, weeping, cries of agony, silent during that short storm of violence, now sang as if it had never happened. They were singing out in the meadow—larks, more than likely.

Charlie Potts came back with Packwood's pistol belt—fancy tooled Mexican leather, two holsters, the revolvers (short-barreled Colts) still in the leather. He had the whip as well.

"Put it on," Lee said to Packwood, nodding to the

gunbelt as he took the blacksnake from Charlie.

"Don't do no more than that, mind," Ford said, still aiming his revolver at the man. "Don't get no hurry-up notions."

"I won't put that on," Packwood said, as if the gunbelt had never belonged to him. "Mister Mathews . . ."

"Put it on," Lee said, "or I will hang you from a tree."

"With rope," Sid Sefton said. "I'd like to see this fatty dancin' in the air."

"You are my witness, Mister Mathews," Packwood said. "Under threat of death." And reached out and took the gun belt from Charlie Potts and slowly buckled it on. He kept his hands away from the holstered Colt's. "I won't fight you, Morgan," he said. "No matter what you do."

One bird, a lark, Lee supposed, had flown in close to them, singing a long ascending trilling song. Very pretty. It seemed to Lee that Packwood—so close to death, since there was no chance that Sid or Charlie would let him live, even if he should outdraw, outshoot Lee—it seemed to Lee the man should be concerned, frightened, at least troubled in his mind now.

No such thing.

Packwood stood staring dully at him, at them all, bulky, and bulkier now with his gun belt strapped around him, his thick, strong hands hanging easy at his sides. A black bear someone had half tamed and brought into human company.

It came to Lee that Packwood, much like an animal, though a clever animal, had no real notion of ever dying. No conception of it—and so was unafraid, only cautious of pain and harm.

"You men go on," Lee said. "Go tend to those horses—we're going to trail out of here pretty soon. Let 'em out a bunch at a time. Let 'em graze, but see they don't start off running."

The three of them stood stubbornly where they were, Ford still pointing his pistol at Packwood.

"I told you three what to do, God damnit! *Now do it!*"

Sid Sefton shrugged, turned, and walked off, and Charlie Potts walked after him. Ford cut his eyes at Lee.

"This thief could be quick," Ford said.

"Not quick enough. Go on now."

"This Mathews?"

"He stays," Lee said. And Ford uncocked his revolver and slid it back into his holster, turned, and walked away.

"You will not get me to fight you, Morgan. Either take us in or let us go."

Lee relaxed his right hand and, holding the handle, let the slim coils of the whip loose from his grip. The coils spilled free like a girl's unbound hair from the clasp of her lover.

"Oh, dear." Mathews had an unexpectedly deep voice.

Packwood looked at the whip, but said nothing.

"If you don't try for that pistol, Packwood, I am going to peel that red hide clear off you." Lee suddenly drew his right arm back and up. The coils of the whip sprang up in obedience like a snake to the will of a sorcerer, curved into a great near loop and, at a turn of Lee's wrist, leaped out with a hiss to lash Packwood across the face with a sound like a breaking bone.

Packwood stood stock still for a long moment; then slowly he put his right hand up to his face, lightly touching . . . running his fingers along the bright red stripe that had suddenly appeared across his cheek, his nose. The red stripe began to bleed.

As Lee watched, Packwood slowly began to come to terms with the pain that must have frozen his face in fire. Lee saw it in the man's eyes—dark small animal's eyes that now, for the first time, began to seem human.

"Murder . . ." Packwood tried to say. Then, "*Mathews* . . ." But his lips could not quite move to form the words. The blow of the whip had struck them silent.

As Lee saw that Packwood, in agony, had become more of a man and less of a brute. He saw that this killing *would* be murder. And the harder he drove Packwood to the fight and the further Packwood was driven, so much more a man it would be whom Lee killed.

And still no choice. Even balancing Ray Clevenger against all of Packwood's dead—six or seven for sure, others down and badly, perhaps mortally injured—even saying that that balanced out, that Ray Clevenger was paid for, there was still no choice.

Packwood could and certainly would do the Bit harm however he could, however long it took, in court or in ambush. Would most certainly do Lee harm.

"Murder," Packwood managed to say, quite clearly and Lee swung the whiplash again, sending the slender leather braid singing in a looping coil at Packwood's eyes.

Packwood got his right arm up before his face just in time and the tiny loaded tip of the lash licked a piece of skin from the back of his hand and broke Packwood's little finger, snapping it in half so the small white bone shone in a red dangle.

Lee felt himself getting sick of it.

No choice . . .

"I figure," he said to Packwood, as the man, saying nothing more, clumsily wrapped his damaged hand in his bandanna like a small present to be carried in a pocket, "I figure," Lee said, "that you're the get of some drunk micky corporal and a poxed-up Digger squaw . . ." He saw Packwood's eyes grow more human yet. "I do believe," Lee said, "that when I get all that red hide off you, we may see some Irish pig manure beneath it." And he took a long step back to clear the next swing of his whip.

Packwood spoke like a man just waking. "You dog of a white man," he said, "my mother was of the greatest heart . . ." looked as if he wanted to say more, had volumes more to say about his mother and his father and the people among whom he'd grown up—the pain of being a half of everything.

Wanted to say more, but couldn't take the time.

It was a man, however, who drew a revolver with his left-hand gun to shoot Lee down.

For a burly man, a heavy man, a man in great pain from the whip, Packwood was surprisingly quick. It was a draw of strength, though, rather than artfulness, and Lee would have beat him easily at any other time.

He let loose of the whip—left the handle of it hanging in the air—and before it had even time to begin to fall, was drawing the Bisley Colt's.

Lee had the Colt's half drawn, had already picked his spot on the heavy man's chest, when pain like the blow of an ax struck at his side and took his breath and strength away.

The tensed muscles, the sudden convulsion wrenching at the draw, had torn at something in his wound.

Packwood drew and fired, and the bullet marked the right side of Lee's head and knocked him sideways, staggering. Packwood fired again, the explosion louder than it should have been in Lee's ears. It was like a thunder clap. Lee pushed his revolver out at Packwood, fired a shot and missed, and fell to one knee trying to fire another.

The heavy man had only to be calm and deliberate for much less than a second. Only had to be calm and deliberate, as he had always seemed to be, and aim and shoot once more.

But Packwood had given way to feelings and to his long-held rage and he yelled with pleasure and fired too fast, and missed.

Lee, still on one knee—seeing, hearing everything as if he and Packwood and Mathews were standing together at the bottom of a cold, clear spring of mountain water—Lee thought of shooting Packwood in that considered spot on his chest, and did, firing through a haze of gunsmoke.

Lee felt the tickle of blood running down past his

right ear as the slug hit Packwood center and shoved him back on his heels. Packwood didn't seem to realize he'd been hit and was raising his pistol again for another shot, quick and triumphant as before, when Lee fired into his chest a second time, struck a vital, and knocked him down and dying.

Packwood struggled on the ground as if he were wrestling something awful in the grass. He tried to get up, staring blindly at Lee and Mathews. He tried to get up, his heavy shoulders heaving like a bear's, his booted feet scrambling in the grass as if life was waiting for him, waiting only for him to stand again.

He got up into a crouch, finally, grunting with effort, or pain. His broad face had gone yellow as clay.

"*Oh so-naw, oh so-na ineearay . . .*" Something in Indian talk. He was staring hard at a place between Lee and Mathews. There was nothing there but the grove of birches, the wooded hill beyond. Then he put his face down into the grass and fell on his side, muttering and slowly convulsing, drawing his legs up and then relaxing them. His eyes were as shiny as glass.

Lee got up—caught his breath as the pain in his side siezed him again—then, after a moment, walked over to where Packwood lay, leaned down, and shot the halfbreed through the side of the head.

He turned and looked at Mathews who still stood with his hands in the air, looking frightened into wood, and said, "Was that a murder? Or a fight?"

"A fight," Mathews said, screwed up his face like a child, and began to cry. "Don't kill me," he said.

CHAPTER FIVE

THE MOTION of the train woke Lee—a mild shuttling jolt. He stretched out carefully in his seat, yawned, and stretched again to ease his muscles.

Only a slight tightness in his side. The skinny, dirty-fingered doctor in Parker had probed the wound through and through with a thin steel probe with a wad of carbolic soaked cotton on the end. That had been no joy at all at the time, but it appeared to have done the trick. Sometimes still the wound would catch him out if he moved awkwardly or suddenly, or twisted from the hips. But otherwise, it didn't trouble him. In a way, the bullet cut across the right side of his head just above his ear was more troublesome. That pained him in a quick stinging way whenever he smiled, or made any sort of face at all.

"Now, young man," the doctor had said, probing away with his slender length of steel, "Now, young man, I want you to go right on out and get into another fight! It's how I get my custom, fixing up fine young bucks like you think you'll live forever. It makes my business for me!"

"I guess not," Lee had said, clenching his teeth 'till his jaw hurt.

"No?" The skinny doctor had looked disappointed, the sunlight from the open window of his office flashing in the glass of his spectacles. "No? Aw, shucks!"

They'd stayed two days in Parker, resting up, letting the horses rest up. Lee'd talked with Ford, and they'd decided it made sense to spend the money to grain the geldings, making up, in that way, for the go the herd had had in getting through in Roughs.

It was an expense of almost two hundred dollars for the grain for the whole herd and Lee suspected the merchant, a tall man named Michael Bowers, thought him a fool to pay it rather than letting the horses loose past town to graze grass.

But Lee and Ford had talked about it, Lee considering as well what Ray Clevenger might have agreed to (after great argument) in the matter. Lee had no wish to off-load a sad, dull-coated herd of horses at the Oakland station. He had a notion—California being horse-hungry as people said—that the buyers might be right there, waiting. Would telegraph ahead in any case, have a notice printed in the San Francisco newspaper, whatever that might be.

So the grain was bought, freighted out to the stock pens, and fed.

And it picked the horses up like Billy-be-damned. Two hundred dollars well spent. Lee bought traveling feed as well and extra buckets, to see the herd got more than enough water, every horse, in the stock cars for the four days of travel.

"We'll be running them out every chance we get, too," Lee'd said to his people.

"At every damn stop?" Charlie.

"At every considerable stop where we've the time."

"An' loadin' again. Damn."

"Best for the herd. Best for the selling price."

Charlie had sighed and let it be. An easier, less resty Charlie since the fight. That saving shot of his, putting that fellow down in time, seemed to have lanced Charlie's own injury. Likely saved Lee's life, knew it, and was made to feel better about his own folly those years before.

The sun was coming up over low, lush, rolling hills. Grass as short and smooth as a rich city man's rolled house-lawn. A few clumps of trees looking too round and neat to be real trees at all. Sun's heat through the window glass waking buzzing flies along the sill.

California. As pretty and warm-aired as rumor had had it.

And mountains, too. They'd come down through mountains for a day and a night, getting to this lush country. Heading for the sea, now. A chance to see the Pacific Ocean . . .

Oakland in an hour and twenty-three minutes, the conductor had said at breakfast. Enough of a dining-car breakfast (four eggs, sausages, pancakes, and a pot of coffee) to honorably put a man back to sleep in his seat for half an hour.

Lee thought for a moment of another railroad train ride just a few years back. Thought about it—had dreamed about it the first night out, and wakened sweating, with a groan. An Iroquois Indian, mad as a foaming dog and big as a horse. And a much smaller man in a fine dark suit. Murder on that train ride, blood on the platforms of that train . . .

That robbery, those killings, they'd put a scar on him he'd carry to his grave. Made a sore place, a frightened place, maybe. A place where Packwood, crying out in some Indian talk, would always struggle, dying in the grass.

It was time to see to the horses. Seven stock cars, carrying the finest stock-working horses in the west. Good horses, and fought for.

They'd let Mathews off, poor broken-down man; given him the pack horse, Pete, to keep and ride off. Whoever had been holding the rustling party's mounts had long since hightailed it. Told Mathews to bring in some help, some women from his neighbors—some dirt-poors too smart to fall in with Packwood's plans—bring them on back to help their wounded, bury their dead.

Seven men shot dead, not counting Ray. Four others lying wounded and like to die. Others, not hurt so bad, must have run for their lives. Sid was right. It was about the biggest fight—the biggest non-U.S. Army fight, anyway—since Adobe Walls. But a bad business just the same. Nobody'd be making up stories and songs about this fight.

Lee had taken Ford and gone to see the Federal Marshal—one of his deputies, rather—in Parker. Told the whole damn thing; but, just in case, had told it with Mercer Boggs, Mrs. Dowd's lawyer, in tow. Mercer, who ranched outside Parker when he wasn't politicking in Boise, had not been pleased to hear of more violence associated with Catherine Dowd's name. Mercer, a strong shouldered fat man with small sense of humor, was, Lee supposed, a little in love with Catherine Dowd, as most men were who knew her, gray in her hair or not.

Mercer had not been best pleased by this trouble but he had, in his lawyer's way, immediately made the best of it, and had, in the deputy's office, filed strong complaints and criminal charges against the rustlers, individual and in group, who had attacked a drive for gain and murdered a beloved and faithful old wrangler in doing it. Lee enjoying thinking of how Clevenger would have cared for that epitaph.

The federal officer had swallowed all that, more or less, and had agreed, with no enthusiasm, to file charges if any chargees could be found.

"Spiked their guns, by God!" Mercer had said, over beef sandwiches, beer, and pickles at the Blue Bull. Lawyer-like he was now all enthusiastic for his side of a fuss. "Let 'em come to court, now!"

Still, he had earlier congratulated Lee on his foresight in shooting Mister Packwood to death. "A disaffected native with a clever mind is a dangerous opponent in court," he said. "Much sympathy now, for our red brothers since they're safely whipped, and their land robbed." Mercer Boggs had winked an attorney's wink. Bob Clay, the owner and proprieter of the Blue Bull for some years now and before, despite his small size and advanced years, the saloon bully and bouncer, came over to the table and sat with them. He'd heard the news, of course, as had all the town, and, being the owner of a ranchers' and drovers' saloon, congratulated them on their triumph.

"A pack of them, I understand," he said. And, "Damn shame about Ray. I liked that man. Will miss him."

. . . *Damn shame about Ray.* Unfair for a friend to die, somehow, Lee thought. As if they'd taken something away from you, going. Like losing something you owned . . . something valuable. Ray was buried beside their camp under the shadow of that wooded hill. And, of course, would still be alive, if Lee had not insisted on driving the herd through the Roughs.

Lee had at least the cold comfort of knowing what Ray Clevenger would have said of that kind of thinking. "Crap through a cow," he'd have said. "Chewed, shit out, and stepped on."

"Oakland!" The conductor coming through. "Still got almost fifty minutes, Mister Morgan. We'll be side tracked for that before we get in to the station."

"Thank you, Mister Peabody." (Courtesy, compliments of Professor Riles of the Cree County Normal Academy School and later, Catherine Dowd. "No use your acting the perfect rough drover, Lee. We can get all of those we want . . .")

So, "Thank you, Mister Peabody."

And the locomotive had shifted, thumped and rumbled down a different length of track; Lee felt the car he was riding jolt and follow suit, the whole length and body of the train lean slightly into a new shallow curve to the right.

Time to get cracking.

Lee stood up, pulled his buckskin jacket down from a clothes hook, and started back up the aisle. His possibles and saddle bags were with the others' goods on the platform on the second stock car down. Some passengers looked up as he went by—curious about the thin raw scar running above his right ear, likely. But most were busy enough getting their baggage together for the stop, corralling their kids, pulling packages out from under their seats. Glad to be getting off, most of them looked. Been a long trip up into the Rockies, then over them. A long trip on a railroad train.

Lee stepped out onto the passenger car platform, crossed the shifting steel plates to the narrow roof ladder, and climbed it to the top of that car. He knelt on the roof, then carefully stood erect, watching his balance, favoring his side.

From this high perch—rolling, for him, backward through the late spring air—Lee could see for miles across the countryside. Low soft green hills marching away like soldiers to the horizon, and, when he turned his head to look behind him, the small smoke-puffing locomotive, and a group of sheds along an empty siding. In the distance, past him, Lee saw chimney smoke and a blur of brown shimmering in the morning sunlight. Oakland, still miles away.

Up ahead, his men were sitting together, Potts and Sefton, smoking cigarettes, Ford smoking a pipe, and surveying the countryside from the roof of the third car down the line. As he walked along, watching where he put his feet as the stock car roofs shifted with the roadbed underneath, Lee congratulated himself on having hired Ford on. The small man, owl-hooter though he likely had been, was a first class wrangler as well as being good with a gun. No bigger than a country-course jockey and every bit as tough.

And old enough to know some things that Lee had yet to learn. Lee was happy enough to acknowledge that, happy enough to have somebody besides those two young hard-cases, Potts and Sefton, to talk business with. Not that Sid Sefton didn't have the brains for it; he did. But Ford had been around, had seen the elephant, as it were.

They looked around as Lee walked toward them, waved him on. Damned if he was going to get careless and fall off this damned train, just showing off he wasn't scared. Lee took his time.

"Coming in less than an hour," Lee raised his voice a little, over the quick thud and chuckle of the wheels beneath them, the ruffle of the soft breeze blowing past them with the last of the train's speed. They were easing into the siding, beginning to slow to a stop.

To the south, Lee could see a small series of black puffs of smoke rising above the green of the hills into the blue sky. A train up from the south taking their track, more than likely, scheduled in just ahead of them.

"Pretty country," Sefton said. "Real soft, though. Ladies' country."

"Shit—anybody's country, you ask me." Potts. "I'll take it, and I ain't no lady."

"Never will be, either, the way you talk," Sefton said, and hit Potts with his elbow. They commenced a little wrestle on the roof of the stock car.

"You pups knock me off the top of this here car," Ford said, staying where he was and puffing his pipe, "you better learn to fly real quick 'cause runnin' won't be fast enough."

"Settle down," Lee said to them, "and listen up." And they settled down, Sefton having drawn his knife and making as if to cut Charlie's throat with it.

"Now," Lee said, "we'll be in the Oakland station next, right after this other train pulls through, and what I want us to do is to get our herd off quick. Get 'em off in a rush—you'll be trailing them across town . . ."

"Must be some town," Potts said. "Where are their damn pens?"

"North side of town. Buyers will likely meet us at the station, go over with us, watch the horses running."

"You want us runnin' those horses through that town?" Ford, knocking out the dottle from his pipe on his boot sole.

"Not a full-out run, no. But step 'em lively—let those buyers get a look at what they're buying."

Ford nodded, got to his feet, said, "Let's get to it, then," and went to the end of the car, onto the platform ladder and down it, Potts and Sefton trailing along.

Lee started after them, favoring his left side, sore now with balancing himself on the roofs of the moving cars and, glancing back toward the locomotive as the train slowed for its side-track stop, saw a man alone, sitting in a buckboard by the siding sheds. The man waved to him.

"Taylor Malone," the cripple said, and leaned down from the buckboard's seat to shake Lee's hand. Mister Malone had a very strong grip. "Pardon my not climbing down," Malone said, and indicated his legs, covered by a red and green afghan rug. "A disease in childhood."

"Hard luck," Lee said. There was not much more that could be said.

"You'd be Lee Morgan?"

"That's right, Mister Malone."

"Well, Mister Morgan, I am a buyer of horseflesh. Buyer and auctioneer. And I've come out here, stealing a march on my friends, you might say, in order to do a deal with you."

"You want to see the horses?"

"I do indeed."

Lee stood for a moment, thinking about it—and, he realized, had not too long to think. If he off-loaded the herd here just for this one buyer's perusal, then he'd likely have to trail them a few miles on to Oakland—they'd be sweaty and dusted, coming in . . .

The locomotive grumbled and hissed, sitting still down the track. Not much time to make up his mind.

Lee liked the look of Malone—a square-built man with a busted-in nose and an intelligent eye. Liked, too, Malone's coming out first.

"Say—Foooord!"

Lee saw the little wrangler turn in a stock car door to see what was up. Cupping his hands to his mouth, Lee yelled again. "We dump 'em out here! Get 'em out!" and saw Ford nod and duck inside.

In a few moments, as he and Malone watched, the quick broad tongue of a plank ramp came sliding out of the stock car's doorway and Charlie Potts scrambled out to secure it.

Less than a minute after Lee had called, the Spade Bit horses came thundering down the ramp and out onto the meadows of the siding. Car after car, Ford and Potts and Sefton ramped down and chivvied the geldings off, living waterfalls of horseflesh.

"Now, by God," Malone said, "that's a pretty sight!"

Ford was mounted now on Rabbit, a tall sorrel, and was riding out to head the herd, stop its running and dashing and scattering. Diablo was off to the flank, nipping a balky gelding in as if the whole herd were mares, and his own.

"That a stallion?" Malone said.

"Late cut."

"Too late, I'd say," and laughed.

"That's the lot."

Malone heaved himself around on the buckboard seat to watch the geldings run and said nothing for a minute. Then he turned back to Lee. "Well, Mister Morgan, I won't fun you; they are very fine horses, and I don't expect to change my mind checking each one close through a pinch gate—which, however, I shall surely do." He reached down to drape the rug across his lap, and Lee caught a glimpse of shrunken little child's legs wearing a child's high-button shoes. "I propose to offer you a good price for your animals—no better a price, mind, than any other Oakland buyer might. Which is," he added, "a very *good* price, the market being as desperate for sound stock as it is. No sir, my price will be no better than any other man's, but I propose an additional." He looked expectantly down from the buckboard, waiting for Lee to ask what that additional might be.

"And what might that 'additional' be, Mister Malone?"

"I propose, Mister Morgan, to purchase the animals from you on consignment fee simple, meaning that I will buy them at a fair price, then auction them myself for further profit . . ."

"And allow us what percent of that profit?"

"Just so. A solid ten percent."

"You meant fifty percent, I suppose," Lee said, enjoying the exchange, "and mis-spoke."

"Did I say ten?" Malone said with an air of surprise. "Then I did mis-speak. It was twenty-five percent I meant."

"Done," Lee said, and reached up to shake the man's hand. "If your base price is fair."

That afternoon, back of the auction sheds in Oakland, Lee and his wranglers stood silent, relieved for the first time in a long time of any responsibility for horses except for the mounts they rode.

The herd was sold—hide, hair, and fetlocks.

Now, in the soft, pervasive heat of a California early summer afternoon, Taylor Malone, having been carried by two stockyard hands to a perch on a high stool behind a lectern and having shouted and auctioned from there most of the day (his own bought Spade Bit herd coming up near last for sale) at last was silent, his stertorous voice still, as he counted gold cash money onto the lectern counter top.

Lee counted out loud.

$17,000 in gold, on the consignment sale.

$2,463 share of profits.

The gold stood in little stacks, growing under the cripple's agile fingers. The coins as bright as sunshine, even in the shadowed shed.

$19,463 altogether. The most cash, the most gold that Lee and his men had ever seen in one place. And that for 339 horses, the herd having been cut by one animal shot dead in the fight, one split-hooved and stalled until Malone could sell it separate, and one, a broad-backed bay, lost on the drive, the last day out of the Roughs and up to Parker. The bay had mis-stepped crossing Coffin Creek, slipped on a water-slick boulder, and broken its right fore. Had been shot.

Malone sat back on his high stool, finished counting. Lee finished counting out loud a moment later. The small stacks of gold on the stained wood.

"My . . . my . . . *my,*" Sid Sefton said.

"Have we done our deal, Mister Morgan—excepting that split-hoof horse I'll sell for you when it's healed?"

"Yes, Mister Malone, we've done our deal."

They shook on it. "One thing," Lee said. "Where is the safest place to keep this money 'till we pull out of San Francisco?" Oakland certainly didn't seem the place for it. There didn't appear to be too much to Oakland, bar the station, the stock pens, a line of shanty shacks, and warehouses down on the water.

"Were I you," the crippled man said, "I'd keep my cash in the safe at the Palace Hotel. Mister Ralston will replace any cash that might be stolen from their safe, personally, I understand. Also, the safe has a deaf nigger with a shotgun sitting by it through the night, Mister Ralston not liking to replace cash if he can help it." Malone thought a moment. "Of course, if you trust a bank and want some little interest on the gold, I suppose the Italian is as good a banker as any."

"An Italian . . . ?"

"Giannini. He's got what he calls 'The Bank of America.' A good little bank though, I hear."

"The hotel, I suppose, will do," Lee said. "How do we find it over there, after we take the ferry-boat?"

"The most beautiful building in San Francisco," Malone said. "The biggest, too." He shifted awkwardly on his high stool. "Time for me to be getting on to home," he said, "or my wife'll hide my crutches."

"Sid," Lee said, "you and Charlie help Mister Malone out to his buggy."

"Be obliged," Malone said. And, Sefton on one side, Potts on the other, they hoisted the auctioneer up off his stool and carried him, child's legs dangling, out of the shed and into the sunlight and across the yard to his buckboard.

Lee scooped the stacks of gold coins into his purse —a Blackfoot-made drawstring, fashioned from a range bull's ball-bag—and Ford followed them outside.

Out in the yard, a few men still hung about, talking cows and horses, pigs and mules, and hanging on the corral fences for careful look-sees at the Spade Bit horses.

"Fine animals," Malone said, settling himself in the buckboard seat, arranging the rug to cover his legs. "You should be proud of them, Mister Lee. Neither I, nor Henrigue Mendez . . ." (a Mexican, ancient and wrinkled as a baked mud field, who had worked beside Malone checking the herd one by one, as the horses singled through a funnel gate) " . . . no, neither one of us remember seeing any more solid stock for working. They'll be a boon, I can tell you, to half the ranches this side of the Russian River."

"Nice to hear," Lee said. And indicated Sefton, Potts, and Ford. "These are the men who did the work with those horses—these men, and another we lost coming here."

"Yes . . ." Malone said, and sat looking down at the four of them for a moment. "Now . . . now, it is no business of mine, gentlemen. But . . . well, damnit, I think I must caution you." He sighed. "This San Francisco of ours is the finest city in the country, in my opinion—the most beautiful, certainly. But boys, it is also a trap for the unwary."

"Lord, lead me to it!" Charlie said, and Malone smiled.

"Yes, I know," he said, "but just be advised to keep in mind that there are men and women over the bay whose profession it is to rob visitors—even horny-handed drovers and wranglers. And if you're careless, or foolish, they'll do it . . . It is the penalty we pay for *having* a city, I suppose."

He picked up his reins. "So enjoy yourselves, gentlemen, but mind where you go alone, and never accept a free drink on the Barbary Coast." He waved his free hand, clucked up his horses, a spavined old gray named Snorter, and rolled out of the yard and was gone.

On the ferry to the city (and a dirty, sluggish old steam-thumper it was) Lee noticed some passengers staring at his revolver and the weapons his men sported on their belts. He motioned Ford over from the rail where the little man was feeding scraps of bread to a small crowd of hovering gulls.

"Ford," he said, "city police don't care to see pistols worn in sight. Makes them nervous, and they likely have an ordinance against it. Tell the boys to wear their pistols in their shirts, their knives down in their boots, 'till we ride in country again."

Ford nodded, and went to do it.

No need to have trouble they didn't need to have.

Lee walked up front along a narrow side deck below the pilot house. The air was full of the smell of salt water; the ruffling wind that swept across the bay was the wind of the sea, for sure, and sunlight of late afternoon as fully gold as the coins in his purse. Gulls were swinging through the air all around them as the ferry bumped its way across. And there, past the bow, Lee saw, looking close enough to reach out and touch, a city as golden as the afternoon air.

The ferry docked at a landing called Vallejo Street and docked with a mighty crash, at that. Lee led the others ashore through the most amazing crowd—Chinamen by the score in black pants or long silk dresses; a parcel of old trappers, hairy as bears, rambling along a muddy pavement. A police officer, in a tight fitting blue suit of clothes with brass buttons (perhaps a fireman, after all); small, swift mobs of hurrying men—clerks and laborers, men of affairs and lay-abouts with none, and all talking as they walked; shouting, some of them.

And women. Every man seemed to have one by his side, girdled in and padded out above and below. Some of them, when they stepped down from a boardwalk with a jolt, might show not only a flash of ankle, but a jiggle of tits as well under their soft white shirtwaists. Some were out-and-out ladies. Some were not.

"Good Jesus God almighty," Charlie said. "This is split-tail heaven, and no mistake!" He paused where they were walking, up this same street, Vallejo, and looked around like a drunkard in a brewery.

"Save your breath for the climb," Lee said, "and come along." It was a very steep street, and even though they'd left their saddles, bed rolls and rifles locked up at the yards back in Oakland, they still had their saddle bags and possibles to lug along. Lee's side was bothering him a little, too; he had the Bisley Colt's tucked under his jacket and down into his belt there for a cross-draw (and a mighty slow one) and the butt of the pistol was galling him, rubbing against his side near the wound.

Be damn happy to reach this Palace Hotel . . .

At the top of the Vallejo Street, there was a cross street called Kearny, and here Lee stopped a swell in a silk top hat and asked for the direction of the Palace Hotel. The man looked astounded that even a stranger could be that much of a fool, turned, and pointed off toward a very large and handsome building that did not appear impossible to walk to even in cowboy boots.

Lee thanked the dude, and the four of them trooped off toward the Palace Hotel, sweating like blacks in the warm early evening air.

The desk clerk, one of four on duty, looked resigned, if not pleased, when Lee and the others finally limped up to his mahogony fortress. They'd been slow crossing the lobby, since Sid Sefton who ordinarily was difficult to impress had noticed after a few yards that the entire lobby floor was inlaid with silver dollars.

It seemed San Francisco *was* the elephant, at least for the style of flash.

"I want a room," Lee said, "and a room for my men."

The desk clerk was a large well set-up man who did not look like a hotel clerk. "I see," he said. "Say, Pardner," he said more softly, "you *do* know this is the dearest hotel in the city?"

"I don't give a damn," Lee said. "I want . . ."

" . . . a room for yourself, and a room—a suite, I think, rather—for your men." The clerk nodded, and turned to his big leather bound book to check for frees. He looked through it for a while. "We have a fine single room on the fourth floor—fireplace, private bath. And a suite of three rooms, two bedrooms and a parlor, fireplace, private bath, on the third floor." He looked up. "Twenty dollars a night for the single. Thirty dollars a night for the suite." He looked back down at the reservation book, very politely, to avoid shaming Lee if the price should prove too high for them after all. "Would that be satisfactory? I'm afraid it's all we have available."

At the quotation of rates, Lee had heard grunts of surprise from his men standing behind him, gaping at the lobby's silver dollars, marble pillars, solid silver urns for ferns and other indoor plants—gapping as well at the guests, most of whom, male and female, looked sleek as minks.

"That'll be just fine," Lee said. "We'll want those rooms for a few days—maybe a whole week."

The clerk nodded and said, "I believe you'll enjoy your stay here, Mister . . . ?" dipped a pen and held it out.

"Morgan." Lee took the pen and signed in the big book where the desk clerk's large clean finger indicated, then, as the clerk's finger moved to a new location, signed there for his men. Sid and Charlie could write after a fashion, Sid fairly well, but Lee didn't know if Ford could write at all, and wasn't about to see the little man humiliated.

When Lee'd signed for all, the clerk nodded, slid the book away, and brought his hand down hard upon a pretty silver bell. Two boys dressed up in uniforms of blue and gold, with large P's sewn onto the jacket fronts in silver thread, came trotting over to take their baggage and lead them up a flight of stairs as wide as a rock slide.

Lee had given the bell-boy a silver dollar (perhaps encouraged into that extravagance by all those silver dollars patterned into the hotel's lobby floor) and had as a result gotten some swift and thorough service.

His Sunday suit pulled out of his possibles sack with his one fine white shirt, collar and cuffs and taken away by another boy—a *valet* boy, this one (two bits)—to be cleaned, furbished up, and pressed to a fare-thee-well, all for return within the hour. Lee's boots, his only footwear, were tugged from his feet for delivery to another fellow, this one an elderly black man (one bit) who guaranteed to clean, oil, and polish them for return, also within an hour.

A hot bath was drawn for him in a deep and wide tub of fine green gold-veined marble, the water entering in through faucets formed in sterling silver and pouring in steaming (from boilers in the hotel's basement, according to the bell-boy). In the bath, which was for Lee alone as promised, were also a stack of thick white cotton towels and wash cloths; a fresh cake of shaving soap; a fresh cake of English bathing soap; an unopened bottle of Bay Rum; an unopened bottle of Macassar oil; and a brand new long-handled scrub brush with soft bristles. Also, a big sea-sponge—or so the bell boy said—which object could be used for bathing. "It suds up," the bell boy said.

With his Sunday suit gone, his shirt and collar and cuffs gone, his boots gone, and other stuff as well (a Chinese man had come and bowed and taken all of Lee's washing away in a straw basket) with all of this in train, Lee had little left to do but to order up a fine dinner and go into his own private bathroom to crap and piss into a glistening porcelain toilet bowl, wipe his butt with a number of soft paper patches, flush with a pull-chain top tank, and climb down into his green marble (gold-veined) tub of steaming hot water, holding his cake of English bathing soap in one hand, his long-handled scrubbing brush in the other.

Lee had known countless less comfortable moments but, except for those brief periods when he'd been actually lying on top of a girl, none *more* comfortable.

He was in the tub a good while, soaping and rinsing, singing a song called *Big-nose Kate,* and sometimes just lying there, resting. The warm water felt good, soothing, as it soaked the bandage over his wound.

He hadn't heard the knocking on the room door—not surprising, since it was a good knife-throw from his private bathroom, but he did hear the knocking on the bathroom door itself.

"Come on in!"

Ford stuck his head around the door edge, said, "Jumpin' Jesus, yores is green!"

"The hell it is!" Lee said, as the wranglers filed in, hats in hand, as if they'd come to circuit court.

"That color stone in yore bathin' tub, I mean," Ford said, blushing like a girl. "Ours is white, with black streaks in it."

"We got every damn thing down there there is to

have," Charlie Potts said. "It's like a damn Turk's palace—thank God!"

"Some doin's," Sefton said, picking up the bathing sponge from a little table by the sink. "We got one of these. What in hell is it?"

"It suds up the soap."

"Damn—Charlie thought it was somethin' to eat."

"I did like hell!"

"I figured we better come on up, find out was there anythin' you wanted to say . . ." Ford stood, hat in hand, still admiring the green marble tub.

"Not much *to* say," sitting up in his tub, Lee said, something touched by Ford bringing the boys up to hear a lecture from the *patron.* "You all heard what Mister Malone said out at the yards. I figure he knows what he's talking about. If you boys get blind drunk, get into a bad bar or girlie show especially on your lonesome, you may well get into serious trouble. One thing's for sure—you can expect to pay plenty for your pleasure in this town. Somebody offers you a bargain, or something free, you better light out running."

"I guess we can handle our liquor O.K.," Charlie said, "we don't need city people to show us how to do that."

"Not if it's straight liquor," Lee said. "I understand they sometimes drug their whiskey here, to put a man down. And don't get any notions that we're tougher than people city-raised. From the jaw my bell-boy was handing out, they have toughs and hoodlums in this town as dangerous as men can get." Lee'd dropped his scrub brush, and had to fish for it in the foamy water. "So don't any of you go off playing cock-of-the-heap, or likely you'll wake up in an alley with a knife in your back or out on some clipper ship, headed for China."

"We'll step real light, Mister Morgan," Ford said, and behind his back Sid and Charlie exchanged quick comic faces at this formal address. "An' how long are we goin' to be in town?"

"I figure three or four days for the pleasure of it," Lee said. "I don't think much more than that."

The three wranglers trooped out of the bathroom in the order they'd trooped in, and Charlie, last out, stuck his hand back around the door with upraised finger—likely to keep Lee from letting that "Mister Morgan" go to his head.

It left Lee a little lonely when they'd gone. He'd assumed, without thinking of it, that the four of them would go out for their fun together, as he and the Spade Bit hands always had. But that seemed to be coming to an end. Damn if he understood why. He was an owner, not just a hired hand—that was part of it. His father had been a notorious and dangerous man and that violence was in him, and his men knew it. And of course, Catherine Dowd had worked to make something of a gentleman of him. A Rocky Mountain gentleman, anyway.

But it left him a little lonely.

He let some more hot water into the marble tub, rolled and thrashed about in the water—the thing was deep as a horse-trough—then climbed out, his fingertips wrinkled as an old lady's face, toweled himself dry, dug in his possibles for clean bandaging and sticking plaster, bandaged the wound on his side which was looking less red, less inflamed, then shaved while his whiskers were still soft from the bath, wrapped a dry towel around his waist, and walked out of the bathroom just as the valet boy knocked on the room door with Lee's Sunday suit all cleaned and pressed, his collar and cuffs white as snow.

His boots came a few minutes later, smelling of neats-foot oil and black wax polish.

The boy and the old negro tipped again and gone —Lee thought that three days would be about all the San Francisco time they could afford, considering all the tipping a man required to command these luxuries—Lee was more than ready enough to sit down to his dinner. For that, though, he had to wait a few minutes more.

He spent some of that time admiring his room. Twenty-five by twenty-five if it was a foot. And done up in fine mahogany furnishings, including a four-poster bed big enough for three girls and a Jersey cow; fancy blue wallpaper with flowers and birds on it; and two wide windows curtained in dark blue velvet. Lee went to the windows to admire his view, and the view was something, at that. To be sure, it was no vista of the Rockies—did not even hold a candle to the upper pastures of the Bit, if it came to that—but for a city view, it was considerably more than something.

Just down the block stood a mansion looking damn near as big as the Palace Hotel itself. A private residence, though, by the gates and fencing —all fancy wrought iron—and by the classy carriage and four drawn up on the graveled drive. Man must be as rich as old man Dowd to afford that sort of doing. One of the old Forty-niners maybe, that had struck it mighty rich.

The lot next to the big house on that very steep hill, was in its way more impressive still. The lot was empty—was, in fact, more of an excavation than a building lot. There, a great slab of the hillside had been carved away—a chunk of chocolate-dark soil some twenty or thirty feet deep and at least a hundred feet on a side. Looked like a smooth square slice cut out of a giant's chocolate cake. Lee could see the tiny figures of men, laborers digging away at the work, teams of mules, a line of freight wagons parked along the sharp slope, waiting to be filled with soil to carry away.

Another palace would go there, Lee could see. Likely the fellow planned to outdo every other palace on that hill top.

It brought to mind some things that Catherine Dowd had spoken of—of the men out here who moved money and influence as most men moved pay-dirt and cattle. "The riches of the West," she would say, looking out at that great excavation, waiting for its palace, its happy owner.

Made the Spade Bit horse herd look pretty small punkins.

There was a knock on his room door, and it was a fellow in a white coat and black trousers, a fine-dressed waiter, with a large rolling cart bearing Lee's dinner.

The menu (though what use it was, since it only described what was on the cart, Lee couldn't tell) was printed on paper as thick and soft as leather, and a very light blue. Lee read it while the waiter, with an occasional soft clink of silver, soft ringing of fine crystal ware, set out his supper. The waiter seemed not to notice that Lee was wearing only a towel, had some sort of bandaged injury to his left side, and a definite bullet crease scarring the right side of his head, just above his ear. The waiter must have seen stranger than that.

THE PALACE HOTEL PRESENTS

Our small supper

Blue Point Oysters

*

Ptge de Terrapin

*

Brook Trout Almondine

*

Fine Chicken Fricassee
Asparagus *New Potatoes*

*

Loin of Beef — Au Jus
Petit Pois *Acorn Squash*
Creamed Corn *Artichoke*

*

Mixed Salad *Fruit Salad*
Waldorf Salad

*

Peach Melba *Deep Dish Apple Pie*
Chocolate Iced Cream *Fruit Cake*

*

Salted Nuts — Cigars — Cognac

Lee couldn't eat it all, but he gave it a damn good

try. He had to let the *New Potatoes*, the *Acorn Squash*, the *Waldorf Salad*, and the *Peach Melba* go. It saddened him, but it was that, or die where he sat.

Lee couldn't recall lying down before full dark for a nap in his life though he must have done so as a small child. It came as a not inconsiderable surprise, therefore, to find himself coming suddenly awake on a plush blue silk sofa an hour and more after his supper. The richly furnished room glowed in gaslight as he woke, and Lee was off the sofa, towel and all, and into his private bathroom as quick as a cat to check his possibles and the purse full of horse-sale gold he'd tucked in there.

The room waiter or whoever had come in to clear the supper things had either been an honest man, or unambitious. And damn foolishness of Lee's, to go off snoring with a full belly, and a purse packed with gold waiting in the next room.

He went to the windows and looked out into a San Francisco night.

It was a sight to see. They had street gaslights here, the tall posts marching up and down the steep hills, the lamps at their tops shining with golden light. The lamps looked like loops of jewels strung through the night. He could see people down there—carriages, horsemen, but mainly people afoot, strolling through the lamplit darkness of their city.

Lee unlatched a window casement and swung it wide. Cool night air came in and riding with it, that same dark, fresh smell of the sea. Hadn't seen the sea, yet. Hell—hadn't seen a damn thing but the ferry, one steep street, and the Palace Hotel. Wasting time, was what he was doing, lying about, eating, sleeping like a hog in high summer . . .

Lee reached up to a fixture and turned the gaslight higher. The Chinese fellow had returned his washing. All stacked neatly, bound with string, on top of the highboy dresser. Damn! Had been a bunch of hotel people in and out of here—and High-pockets Lee Morgan lying on the sofa dead to the world, his purse in the bathroom, waiting for anyone with a notion!

Lucky—and likely a good hotel, that didn't hire snoopers.

Lee felt the better for the sleep, though. Hadn't dreamed of Packwood. Hadn't dreamed of that big-nosed man, either. Nothing about the fight. Nothing about Ray Clevenger.

A good sleep, and time now to go and do this big town to a fare-thee-well!

Lee Bay-rummed his face and armpits, Macassared and brushed his hair, and then dressed in fresh clean clothes from toe to top, excepting only his Stetson, something battered. Underclothes, clean shirt, boiled collar, cravat, cuffs, stockings and stocking suspenders, dark gray suit trousers, galluses, and a long-tailed gray claw-hammer suit coat. Fine as nine pennies! Lee thought, examining himself in the dresser glass. Damned (the battered Stetson to the side) if he didn't look like *belonging* in the Palace Hotel in San Francisco!

Now, recalling Malone's warnings, a question of weapons.

Usefulness of high-top boots and a long-tailed coat. Short, broad-blade dagger, sheathed, to tuck down into the top of Lee's right boot. And the

Bisley Colt's, grip reversed for a behind-the-back reach, slid into Lee's waistband back under the right tail of the coat, a slow draw being better than none. Lee regretted his whip, but it didn't seem quite the thing to be strutting the town in a gentleman's clothes and have a blacksnake whip coiled over a shoulder.

Not the thing, at all.

Different desk clerks were on duty when Lee came down the wide marble staircase. Two flash young gents were coming into the lobby as Lee went to the desk—a mighty handsome pair of bloods; they looked alike as two fine carriage horses, all duded up in black evening clothes and patent leather pumps, high silk hats, cloaks and canes, and diamond stick-pins in their cravats. One, the taller man, had ears on him like batwing doors, still the sports were a fine pair for all that and had, besides, two women with them who didn't have the look of wives. Almost ladies, the women looked, in low-cut dresses so their titties showed. And more than half drunk, Lee thought, the four of them.

The man with the ears came up to the desk while Lee was standing there, walked almost straight getting up to it, nodded at Lee in a friendly way, and asked for his and Mister Stanford's keys. Lee had already handed his $18,800 over (minus the men's monthly wages and a solid one-hundred dollar bonus each, for the drive and the fight and sheer go-to-hell San Francisco money and minus more than three hundred dollars out of his own share for the same honorable purpose) and was waiting for his receipt.

"Good evening to you," said the ears, in a courteous manner, while a clerk searched the pigeon holes for his room key and his friend's.

"Evening."

The sport looked Lee up and down. "Not a city man, I see."

"No."

The desk clerk found the fellow's keys, and handed them to him. Across the lobby, Lee could see the girls giggling at some sally of the other fellow's.

Ears, however, stayed at the desk for a moment, jingling the room keys idly, staring at Lee with bloodshot hazel eyes.

"Cattleman?"

"Horses."

"Ah . . . ah, horses. We can certainly use some decent horses; this damned fever . . ."

"We just brought you a bunch."

"Damn good of you—pleasure or working?"

"Working."

"All the better," the young gent said. He had been leaning more and more heavily on the edge of the desk, but now he straightened abruptly, and stood up. "Pardon—a little the worse . . ." He stared hard at Lee again. "You seem a decent fellow," he said and, before Lee could decide whether to take offense, added, "Out on the town, are you?"

"Yes," Lee said. The other clerk, a bald man with a waxed mustache, was coming back with his receipt. "Yes, I intend to paint the town a little bit."

The young man with the ears laughed. " 'Paint the town,' by God," he said. "Well, sir, this is *the* town to paint!" And threw a glance for Lee's benefit at the two lookers across the lobby. "And I'll tell you what, Mister—what the devil is your name?"

"Lee Morgan."

"Well—I'll tell you what, Mister Morgan, you just go see the 'Bella Union' first, understand? Charlie here will direct you, won't you, Charlie—way to the Union?"

"Yes, sir," the desk clerk said and slid Lee's receipt across the desk top to him. "I certainly will."

"And of course, there's the Coast, there's 'Blackie's.' Mighty rough, though, Blackie's. Still—are you a dangerous man, by any chance?" This last was asked with apparently no offense meant—for information.

"I might be, I suppose," Lee said, "if given no choice."

The sport put his head back and roared at that. " 'If given no choice,' huh?" He'd laughed himself scarlet in the face, and was looking more unsteady. "Well, then, go on to 'Blackie's,' if you have the stomach for it. Right down Pacific to the Coast. Ask anyone there . . ."

"Thank you," Lee said, and the young man suddenly put out his hand.

"William Hearst," he said, staring hard at Lee to keep him properly in focus, "and mind you be careful, now, violent man or not."

"Thank you for the advisories," Lee said, and the sport nodded and swung clumsily away from the desk to stride over to his friends, the room keys jingling in his hand.

The desk clerk gave Lee his directions—to the

"Bella Union" first, then, in a lower voice, to the other snuggery situated where Broadway met Kearny Streets. The directions given, the clerk wished Lee luck and turned to other business.

The wide, high-ceilinged lobby was crowded now with men and women dressed for evening. No sign of young Hearst and his friends, likely already halfway to their rooms with the women. Oysters, champagne, and bare-titted women . . .

Lee'd had his own order of Blue Points for supper —time to go get the rest.

He crossed the lobby floor, boot heels ringing on yard after yard of inlaid silver dollars, of blocks of matched marble edging the wide double doorway, and out and down the steps into the night.

CHAPTER SIX

HE WALKED into a bright confusion of light, the sounds of hard heels on pavement, the light rattle of rigs jouncing over cobbles and rock filled roads, the light, mean crack of coachmen's whips, the small red lamps on the carriages sailing down the streets like magic. Men and women hustled past him, moving from shade into gold as they walked under the gas lamps. Soft talk, shouting, further down on Pacific Street—and always the breeze coming up through the city, bringing with it the breath of the sea.

Lee felt as if not only a great city but all the world was waiting for him and knew, in a sudden moment of knowing, how fortunate he was to be young and strong and to have all this before him.

He walked to Kearny Street and started down a long, long hill, walking down into busier crowds, more noise of voices, carriage wheels, hoofbeats on cobblestones. Jostling crowds on the sidewalks, all sorts of people, all sorts of faces under the lamp lights. Those lights gradually joined by more and still more light—gas light, oil lights, kerosene lanterns strung across narrow doorways, batwing doors, red painted double doors above high stoops. Chinese lanterns, too, hanging in entranceways, some showing small red dragons chasing small green dragons endlessly around the glowing shade.

Smells . . . odors from everywhere. Oriental things, incense of rare woods and herbs, smoky, sweet, hanging in the cool salt air. Well-known stink of stale beer, spilled rye whiskey . . . cheap perfume and toilet water.

Light blazing from both sides of the street now, until the dark pavement was white with it—and full of sound. Screams and pleasant laughter. Music . . . louder and louder as he walked down the hill.

The crowd was thicker here, swirling in and out of variety theater doors, saloon doors, alleyways, basement dives, side-step gates, and four French doors flung wide open into a place called "*The Plaisance.*"

The music now came thundering and tinkling, humming and tumpeting from every blazing window. Pianos, pianolas, players, cornets, string orchestras, drums and clarinets, a chorus of roaring drunks singing in a language Lee had never heard before. Curses . . . women's screams.

Lee heard a revolver shot, a little way away—the next block, maybe. And a wind coming in off the sea, heavy with fog, sharp with salt.

The Barbary Coast.

Lee saw a big sign lit by gas light torches down the block on the other side of the street. *The Bella*

Union. A noisy crowd packed the sidewalk outside the place—a number of gentlemen and some women that might have been ladies, too. Heavy veils on those ladies.

Lee cut across the street, dodging a hired hack and paying no heed to the coachman's cursing and eased his way into the crowd. He'd been right about the ladies—could smell the odor of soap and freshness, lavender water and flower *sachets.* Ladies—and come to see some raw doings, apparently. A man or two with each one, of course, the men dressed to kill and carrying heavy, gold banded sticks that likely *would* kill if some drunk or tough got out of line.

Lee, half a head taller than most and not having to stop to talk with friends, or try and goggle through a veil to see if Mrs. This-or-That were slumming, was able to squeeze his way through to the ticket booth, wait while a man who *wasn't* a gent and his light of love bought tickets and went into the theatre lobby, then purchase his own—twenty-five cents for the orchestra, a dollar for a private box.

Lee sprung for the buck, pushed through the lobby doors (a bruiser in a yellow checked suit took his ticket and tore it) and found himself in a huge mirrored bar room with a double door to the theatre outlined by pink velvet curtains in the opposite wall.

There were certainly a thousand people in the room lined along two fifty-foot bars set at either side wall, and packed around crowded four-chair tables through the center of the room. Lee looked across the saloon, trying to catch a glimpse of his men. Damn foolishness, of course—no reason they would have come to the "Bella Union," out of all the dives in San Francisco.

Truth was, he missed being with them.

The *Boss;* the *Chief;* The *Old Man;* The *Stud Duck. The Lonely Jackass* would be more accurate.

Lee stopped looking and plunged into the crowd following a line of better dressed citizens (including two of those carefully veiled ladies) as they wound their way around tables full of drunken clerks, laborers, hoodlums and whores, heading toward the theatre entrance. Lee was some relieved when this dandy bunch made tracks beside the right-hand bar and he had just time enough to catch a barman's eye (there were at least six of them laboring away behind the gleaming mahogany) and to shout out an order for a straight shot, rye. The barman nodded, turned to pour it, and Lee shoved past a tall man to get a touch of the bar.

The tall man shoved back and turned a long busted-nose horse's face to Lee with a frown. He was Lee's height, maybe a half inch over, and wore blue jean trousers and a knit shirt, yellow, with the sleeves cut off. The fellow's long arms were roped with veins and muscles, and patterned over the sun-blackened skin every visible inch were blue ink tattoos: flying birds, mottoes, patriotic and otherwise, a bigger bird—seemed to be an eagle—and, down his left arm, a naked girl with her tongue stuck out.

Lee thought the fellow a sailorman—at least he looked the way Lee had heard them described. Looked more than fairly tough, too.

"Say, you dumb fuckin' cow-screwer," the man

said (Lee noticed a shorter, broad-faced article, another sailor apparently, standing just behind his comrade at the bar) "who the fuck you think you're pushing?" The long-faced sailor frowned into a snarl. "Well, mother-fucker?"

Lee stepped back a little into the crowd, to give himself more room. "Oh, please, Mister," he said, "don't *strike* me!"

For a moment the sailor's mouth hung open, then he started to grin with pleasure—and suddenly stopped, and stared at Lee hard. Then he said, "Very funny," and turned back to the bar.

The bartender, who had stood waiting with Lee's whiskey in his hand looking not at all interested in the outcome of the dispute, then reached Lee his drink, took two bits from him, and drifted on down the bar toward a crowd of lumbermen calling for service.

The delay had cost Lee his lead steers, and as he turned from the bar to force his own way through the crowd to the theatre entrance, he heard the sailor's friend, behind him.

"Why in hell didn't you paste that asshole, Macky?"

"*You* paste him," the tall sailor answered him. "I'll watch."

As he half-drifted, half-shoved his way toward that pink curtained doorway, finishing his whiskey as he went, Lee had a few chances to look around this astonishing saloon. The room was so big—considerably larger than the lobby of the Palace Hotel—that the thick haze of cigar smoke that hung just below the ceiling seemed as dense and lowering as a storm cloud. The noise that rose to it was a steady roar of voices in which even occasional shouts and women's screams were buried. So big that in a far corner Lee could see a five instrument band playing in what apeared to be dumb show for a group of waltzers. He could not for the life of him catch even a whisper of that music above the tumult.

There were cow hands, ranch hands in the place. Lee noticed a few of them. But most of the customers were sailor men, lumberjacks, and city people—clerks, train men, and thugs. These last, with faces as blunt and savage as fighting dogs', wore workmen's caps pulled low over their eyes, tight green or yellow suits—some, though, in trousers, turtle-neck sweaters and high-crown plug hats—and they had, most of them, women with them—whores or doll-mops (some of these young and quite pretty under their face paint, others as raddled, odd, and vicious looking as their men).

A girl at a table he was just passing glanced up at him, winked, and made a kissing sound at him, smacking her lips. She would have been a pretty girl, but her left eye was white and blind. Two men at the table with her looked up at Lee; one of these men was nothing much, a fat man with spit curls across his forehead, but the other was a slight young man with pleasant blue eyes who also made a kissing sound at Lee, and opened his right hand on the table to show a closed straight razor in it.

Lee let it pass and continued on his way. Practically at the theatre door now. No use getting into a killing scrape—a cutting scrape, for sure—and him not having seen the town at all.

There was another bruiser at the pink curtains, and Lee showed him his torn half of ticket, walked through the doorway, and found himself in a sort of bright scarlet and gold heaven, an oval high ceilinged room with tiers of gilt framed boxes set in a horseshoe curve facing a fine painted theatrical curtain. (The subject of the painting was a little hard to make out—there were naked babies with bows and arrows, grown-up naked women, a naked man with goat horns on his head, and a number of pink and gray mourning doves flying above all.)

A small, plump girl in a short skirt that showed her legs came bustling up to Lee and asked to see his ticket stub. She had some sort of cap perched on top of mouse brown hair. It looked like an antimacassar more than anything.

"Hi, Tex," she said, "How're they hangin'?" She examined the stub. "Come on with me." and led off at a fair trot to a narrow flight of stairs to the right of the door, and up these. Lee following behind her, watching her small sturdy haunches churning up the steps, thought this girl would make a more than satisfactory cutting pony were she a little bigger and capable of a winter coat.

The girl led him up to the third landing, then through a narrow, white painted door, down a corridor no wider, and through a set of canvas curtains painted with a dubious sunset into a small velvet lined box the color of a Valentine card. The only furniture there, all there was room for, was a small cushioned settee, not too uncomfortable.

"Can I get a drink?" Lee said.

"Sure can, sucker," said the cutting pony, "but

not from me." Turned, showed her round little calves, and disappeared back through the canvas sunset.

Company gone, Lee settled onto the little sofa and looked out into the *Bella Union Variety Theatre.* This second room was damn near as big as the bar had been and considerably more civilized. From his box, Lee could look down into the pit where a considerable orchestra, led by a skeleton of a man in black evening clothes, was already tuning up with a fair enough racket, and across the orchestra to the three tiers of boxes opposite. A number of veiled ladies and their dashing escorts, over there. One of the ladies had opera glasses to her eyes (the veil drawn up), and was looking back at Lee as he stared at her. After a moment, this lady waved to him.

Some bored, Lee thought, these good women must be, with nothing much to do but order their servants to clean this and that, and then go carriaging out to tea. Not surprising they took a night on the town, some of them, when they could get an escort, husband or husband's friends, to take them.

Not all the boxes, though, were filled with fancies. Most of them held bits of the same crowd that had filled the bar room in front, including some toughs buisily engaged in shouting to their friends below in the orchestra—and, in the case of one, climbing up on a box rail to pretend to open his trousers and piss on the crowd below. This was taken with great merriment and pretended panic by the mob directly beneath him.

A good natured bunch, all in all. Lee, the short whiskey warm inside him, settled back to enjoy whatever show it was the orchestra was now introducing with a sudden fanfare of trumpets and a long roll of drums.

The huge curtain shook, sagged, then slowly, as stately as could be, rose foot by foot three stories high and out of sight. The stage set was revealed to be an Irish village—very true to life, as far as Lee could tell—looking very small and muddy, with a row of thatched houses about big enough for a large dog to live in.

There was tremendous applause—either for this stage set, or the orchestra's loud and jaunty Irish music (a jig of some kind), or for the three men and three women seated in a wide semi-circle down front of the little row of false houses. They were dressed as Irish people except for the women's short skirts—the men sporting high-top green hats, green coats with big buttons, and knobby blackthorn sticks.

The applause kept on for some time, and men in the audience began to shout: "*Harrigan . . . Harrigan . . . HARRIGAN!*" at the top of their lungs. When the yelling reached a terrific pitch, the actor seated at the far left suddenly stood up to tremendous cries of joy from the audience and began to dance and sing, or rather, to dance and tell a story in a high-pitched sing-song voice. He was speaking in such a thick Irish brogue that Lee at first couldn't make out what the fellow—Harrigan, apparently—was saying. But gradually, listening carefully and taking some cues from the crowd's laughter, Lee came to understand that Harrigan was telling his own story in the person of a man named Micky O'Toole, a small farmer and fine fellow who'd had the ill luck to fall in love with his pig.

This sad story Harrigan half told, half sang, all the while doing the oddest, most comic little dance across the stage and back again. The pig's name was Emma, and Harrigan, recounting how they'd met, stopped his prancing to stand and face the audience, and sing, in a fine deep voice, a ballad to her charms.

The words to this were serious, and so delivered, which made it funnier than what had gone before. Harrigan—O'Toole—sang of the various flowers in the garden, dawn-blooming, day-blooming, night-blooming, whose fair scents his Emma rivaled in any hour of the twenty-four. "*No nasturtium, nor posey, nor rosebud fine . . . may rival the perfume of that daisy of mine.*"

Great applause. Several garters thrown onto the stage as Harrigan finished the ballad.

Then one of the actresses rose up and either her brogue was less authentic, or Lee was getting used to the way of it, since he understood pretty soon that she was O'Toole's fiancee, jilted now for a pig, and mighty furious about it.

As this girl (very pretty, with dark blonde hair done up high on her head) advanced from her chair and began to dance and sing, a roar of "*Adah . . . Adah . . . ADAH!*" almost as loud as the cheering for Harrigan came rolling down over the footlights. This pretty girl then danced a ring around Harrigan, poking some mighty raw fun at him for loving the pig, including some notion of the smallness of his dicky-bird, that had, Lee noticed, the veiled ladies across the theatre orchestra rocking with laughter in their boxes. And as these two danced and clowned and sang, the other actors on stage played tambourines and clapped and sang along, keeping up the fun.

Now the girl was making up to the farmer—flipping up her skirts "*to give you a smell of fresh fish . . .*" and offering various other inducements in order to rope him in again.

This apparently worked, because soon the farmer and his girl were singing a love duet, he full of apologies about being such a fool . . . thanking his stars the priest never found out, and so forth. Then at the climax to this song, just as they fell into each other's arms, a large white pig came hurtling across the stage, squealing to beat the band. The pig had a large pink ribbon around its neck made into a bow.

At this, the farmer instantly dropped the girl (she fell on her buttocks, her skirt in the air), turned, and run after his true love, calling "*Emma . . . Emma, me darlin'!*" And the house roared, much pleased.

There was more of the same, with the actors asking for suggestions from the audience for acting-skits or songs and doing every one with no hesitation at all. No matter what the song—even some in Swedish, and one in Russian—at least one of them knew it and could sing it well. It was quality entertaining, and no mistake. And was enlivened, every now and then, by the pig's entering again at a run, squealing, and always pursued by Harrigan, running himself in the style of a man with a mighty hard-on that he is trying to conceal.

The audience howled every time he and the pig ran across the stage and so did Lee. He rocked back and forth on the small settee, trying to favor his left side, which ached the worse every time the pig ran by with Harrigan in pursuit, and Lee couldn't help laughing. Trying to stop laughing only made it worse.

Toward the end of the show—there'd been a sort of interlude, with the orchestra playing jass music in a sort of fast, jumping rhythm—Lee and the rest of the audience was forced to start laughing and applauding all over again when one of the older actresses, a huge fat woman, who must have weighed three hundred pounds, heaved herself out of her chair and, banging on her tambourine, did the damndest galloping dance that Lee had ever seen. "The Cow!" the audience yelled. "*Go—the Cow!*" And go the woman did, flinging her legs about like a girl (and these legs as thick as a man's waist) prancing, galloping, leaping around the stage as if she were on wagon springs, her short dress flying up around tree trunk thighs and buttocks big as a bull's. And yet the fat woman got up into the air and flew, kicking this way and that before she landed with a crash, took a run like a grain-heavy goose's, and launched herself into the air again all in time to the rattle and thump of her tambourine, the merry fiddling from the orchestra pit. She grinned at the audience, rolled her eyes, winked, and made all manner of funny faces and most of this sailing by in midair.

She was such a jolly creature, it was impossible not to love her, and Lee cheered and clapped her dancing on as loudly as any drunken hoodlum in the crowd. Men were standing to throw money onto the stage, and flowers, and still she thundered on, her feet, oddly small in spangled slippers, twinkling as fast as sparrows' wings as she danced a final circle round the stage, her tambourine jangling above her head, her round, rouged face beaming.

A tremendous climax, a thundering Spanish step two-step, and she came to a stop, shuddering like tapioca pudding, afloat in an ocean of applause.

Lee, feeling wonderful, battered his hands sore for the Galloping Cow, and exchanged pleased glances with people in the box next to his—a banker-looking man and his wife. All the audience seemed one happy family together—a great, single, very pleased person. Lee never expected to enjoy theatricals so much.

And then, at the end of the show, when the orchestra was sawing away at a sea chanty tune and some people were already getting up out of their seats to stretch for the long interval, Harrigan once more appeared in close pursuit of the pig and chased the squealer down off the stage, through the orchestra pit, and straight up the aisle through the crowd. He was promising marriage as he ran out of sight.

The house gas lights and the bright limelights at the front of the stage were turned down after this, and the theater darkened quite a bit. It was restful, after all the light and music and cheering, and Lee sat back at his ease, looking out over the crowd below, thinking whether to stay for the next show or to head out and see more of the town.

He was considering going out to the bar for a drink—some cold beer would go down well—and to smoke a cigar and then decide whether to come back in, when he heard someone talking out in the corridor, some people walking by and, a moment later, the canvas curtains to the box were pushed aside, and a girl in a short dress looked smiling in.

"Hi, handsome!" she said. "If you're half the sport you look, you'll be ordering an ice-cold bottle of French champagne!" and stood perched on the step down into the box, beaming at him through a mask of face paint.

At first Lee thought the girl a tart that just painted uncommon thick, then he realized she was an actress—it was theatrical makeup on her face.

"Well?" She held her head cocked to one side. "It's nice and cold." She gave him a considering look, bit her lip, and said, "I . . . I can do a lot of cuddlin' for a bottle of champagne."

"Can you?" Lee said, amused. It appeared that the *Bella Union* made its real money in liquor.

"Yes," she said, and seemed to blush. It appeared that she was a good actress. A moment after he thought that, Lee recognized her. She was the girl who'd played Harrigan's fiancee on the stage. Knowing that, he looked at her again and realized how clever the owners of the *Union* were, to send their actresses selling, rather than some common tart.

The girl—*Adah*, the audience had called her—was no great beauty. Her nose was a little big, her eyes not beautiful, either—an ordinary girl's gentle brown eyes. But she had a marvelous body . . . long strong legs like the legs of a young thoroughbred mare. And plump little breasts poking half out of her dresstop. She had, above all, that special quality about her—either natural, or the result of Lee's having seen her robed in light, dancing and singing to the applause of a thousand men and women—a quality of being more *present* than most women . . . of having wonderful secrets about her, somehow.

The girl stood perched on the step as if she were frightened of him (likely a useful pose with sentimental drunks) and waited to see what he would say.

"Is it real champagne? Or fizz water?"

"Oh, it's real. It's the goods," she said. "An' it'll only cost you five bucks, Mister."

"And some cuddling . . ."

She appeared to act another blush and some confusion for him. "That's right," she said.

"Then bring it up." And she was out through the curtain and gone.

It appeared Lee was about to taste some of the pleasures of the town. He was not such a rube as to think a drink-peddler, actress or not, was intending to provide an ass-hauling with every sale; still, it might be fun to try his luck with this charming Adah. She was daisy enough to be worth any man's trying.

He leaned forward, resting his forearms on the box rail, watching the crowd below, the orchestra now playing some slow song. Some of the audience had left. A lot more, though, staying for the next show. Some were swaying back and forth, picking up the song the orchestra was playing—"Only A Bird In A Gilded Cage . . ." singing it together—and sounding pretty good, too. Good as a big church choir. Lee supposed it was a custom here for the theater audiences to sing together. Nice custom.

A few of the veiled ladies were still sitting across the theater fanning themselves, veils fluttering, in the big room's heat. If the champagne was cold and good, if the actress, Miss Adah, was agreeable, too, maybe Lee'd stay for the next show as well. After all, there was not all that much hurry about doing the town. Days still to do that. Lee wondered if Harrigan would keep chasing the pig right on through the evening. Supposed he would, and supposed it would be laughed at as long as the actor cared to do it. Not every man can chase a pig, pretend a hard-on, look horny and ashamed at once and do all that a dozen times, and each time different, and each time funny. Might stay and see the next show . . .

Looking across the theater, Lee noticed that the curtains had been drawn across several of the third tier boxes. Privacy for hanky-panky—with the actresses and other ladies. It seemed a good idea.

He stood up, found the edge of the red velvet drapes gathered at the side of the box's front, untied a velvet cord, and drew the curtains across. The little box was nearly dark now, lit only by a small gas lamp on the wall. Civilization, Lee thought, and was mighty pleased about it.

The girl came bustling through the canvas curtains at the back, balancing a tin tray holding an ice bucket with a bottle of champagne stuck down on it, and two long-stemmed glasses, each with a folded napkin tucked inside.

"Here we are!" She had a throaty voice, particular

and personal at once. Lee saw again what a pretty girl she was; marvelous legs—what he could see of them—full, firm little breasts lifting almost out of her corselet (Lee could see a faint golden dusting of down on the white rounds of them) and the same soft wheat-gold dusting along her slender forearms as she worked busily to loosen the champagne cork.

Lee stood up, took her by the elbow, took the wet, cold bottle from her, and sat her down on the settee. "I've opened champagne bottles before," he said to her. "You just take your ease there, Miss Adah." And as he levered the wine cork loose with his thumbs, smiled and talked with her to put her at ease. He saw no use in being coarse, even with a bought girl.

"Mister Harrigan is certainly the best comic actor I've ever seen," he said to her. "A lot more accomplished than the road-show people we're used to in Idaho . . ."

"Yes," the girl said, "he's wonderful." Her eyes, a light, clear blue, like a child's eyes, widened with pleasure. "Did you know, Mister . . ."

"Morgan. Lee Morgan."

"Did you know Mister Harrigan was just a ship caulker—a laborer? They pushed him on stage for a joke just three years ago and he took hold and sang and danced and told those Irish stories and people loved him!" She sat neatly upright on the little sofa, apparently considering that great and sudden triumph. "He became a star right away," she said.

"A star—meaning he's the best?"

She glanced up at Lee. "Well—he is the best, the

best in San Francisco, anyway. But a *star*—that means people will come and see a show just because he's in it."

The cork came out of the wine bottle with a hollow popping sound and Lee had to go some quick to get the first foam of wine into the glasses instead of onto the box's carpeting.

"I'd say," he said, "that you're something of a star yourself."

"Oh, I'm not," the girl said.

"If you're not—not yet—then I'd say you soon will be, the way this crowd was cheering you. And as much as I enjoyed watching you."

The little actress blushed. "Well," she said, "maybe I will be, someday."

Lee handed her her glass of wine and noticed that she barely tasted it. He took a sip himself. Lee'd had French champagne more than once in the *Bull* in Parker, and was surprised to find that this wine was very good, maybe the best he'd had. The *Bella Union* didn't cheat its drinkers on their choice.

"That's good wine," he said, and sat down beside her. "It isn't as sweet as some."

The girl smiled, but shyly, and seemed to sit up straight. When Lee reached for the bottle to pour himself a second glass and to offer her a bit more, she quickly covered her glass with her hand, and shook her head. "I . . . I'm not supposed to drink a lot when I work," she said.

Lee put the bottle down, smiled back at her, and put his arm around her. Her shoulders felt small, soft and strong at once. His left hand barely brushed the smooth naked skin above her arm.

"You did," Lee said, "mean what you said about some loving?" He gently stroked that smooth naked shoulder. "I surely hope you did, for I've never seen a girl more lovely than you are. You're worth more to a man, even for a little while, then all the champagne there is. More than any expensive things at all . . ."

Adah blushed again, but she didn't ease herself into the circle of his arms. She still sat upright as a soldier. She had caught her lower lip in her teeth, nervous as a child.

"Oh, I meant it," she said, not looking at him. "You seem a nice man. Nicer than . . . some men who come here." She looked at him and smiled.

Lee put his hand gently on the nape of her neck just under the rich weight of her upswept hair. That mass of dark yellow hair seemed too heavy for her slender neck. Still—she was not perfectly beautiful. Her nose was snubbed as a country girl's, and her teeth, white as writing paper, were uneven. But there was this . . . special thing about her, as if she held herself to be valuable. It made her different from most saloon tarts.

He gripped her neck a little more firmly, leaned toward her, and kissed her lightly just behind her ear. It was like kissing warm, soft glass, so fine her skin was there.

She stiffened under his hand, though, and said, "Please . . ."

The canvas curtain suddenly rustled. There was a little rapping at the door frame and the stocky girl, the little cutting horse who had shown Lee to his box at the start of the show, stuck in her head, antimacassar cap and all, and said to the actress, "Adah, Mister Hawkins wants you. You come quick, now!" and ducked her head back through the curtains and disappeared.

"Oh, *darn* it!" the actress said, as though she meant it. But Lee felt an easing of her muscles, of relief at the interruption, under his hand at the back at her neck.

As sure as God made little green apples, he thought, that call came in too handy.

"Who's this Hawkins?"

"Darn it—he's my boss. I don't know why he wants me, but when he does want to see us, we surely have to hop!"

And she made to get up.

Lee might have let her, too, if she hadn't been so artful about it. He knew the ticket girl worked this trick with Adah as a routine thing. Gull the customer into ordering champagne with a promise of some sport, then go back on that promise by a trick. "Mister Hawkins" had called for no one, that was certain sure.

As the girl started to rise, Lee tightened his grip on the back of her neck and held her. Ordinarily, he might have let the matter go. A fellow came to a joint or den with some reasonable expectation of being gulled, taken for at least something extra where liquor and women were concerned. It was part of the business; and only a farmer or a fool expected otherwise.

"Mister . . ." the girl said, a little frightened, and tried to twist out from under Lee's grip.

Ordinarily . . .

And what was different here? The girl, perhaps, and the long drive and railroad ride. The fight they'd had . . . More than likely it was the girl herself. There was more to her than most; she seemed—seemed . . . *concentrated*, somehow.

Lee did not intend to let her go.

He'd asked if her promise was still meant and she'd said yes.

Let her abide by it.

CHAPTER SEVEN

"MISTER . . . PLEASE . . ."

Lee gripped the back of her neck harder as he might the nape of a farm dog, to hold him. The actress had half risen. He gripped her and forced her down.

"You have business with me to complete, Miss," he said. "I don't at all take to being cheated of a promise."

She twisted under his hand, her eyes wide, frightened. "Oh, *please* don't! I really have to go. I *have to* . . ."

"No," Lee said, "you don't—and you won't." In one motion he stood and putting his weight behind his hand on her, forced the girl down onto the sofa stretched full length.

She gasped and tried to kick out at him. Lee saw her mouth open to scream, her terrified eyes, and brought his other hand down firmly onto her face, covering her mouth with the heel of his palm, clamping her nostrils shut with his thumb and forefinger.

Burking, it was called. Why, Lee didn't know. It had been shown to him by a cadet in a Parker saloon. "A pacifying clutch," the fellow, a tall, weary-looking drink of water in a fine brown suit, had called it. "Not too harsh, and not held too long," he'd said. "But it's a marvel with the girlies—it pulls the starch out of them neat as anything."

Terrified now, the little actress fought and kicked beneath Lee's leaning weight. The girl's long strong legs—dancer's legs—kicked wildly out. He saw she wore frilled underthings, was not bare-cunted as whores so often were. Her eyes rolled. She must think he meant to kill her, had gone mad and meant to kill her, for she fought as if she fought for her life, clawing frantically at the sleeves and front of his clawhammer coat, trying to strike up at his face. Lee felt her small mouth move under the weight of his smothering palm trying to bite, to twist away—trying for one breath of air.

He leaned down harder, holding her, putting his knee into her corsetted little belly, forcing her head down into the settee's soft cushions, keeping her mouth tight covered, the delicate nostrils pinched shut.

Her face was red now, suffused with blood as she thrashed and struggled, kicked out desperately. As he moved to keep her down, keep her smothered and silent, Lee upset the champagne bottle on the carpet. The wine foamed out.

Now the girl was heaving under his hands like a little horse, trying to buck her way free, her head thrown back, slender neck flushed, corded with veins as she struggled to breathe. Her long legs were spraddled wide, kicking aimlessly as a dying deer's might, heart-shot. As Lee, sweating with effort, bore down upon her, staring into her face, he saw her eyes slowly roll back into her head.

She heaved beneath him only once more, her small hands clutching hard at his coat's fabric. Then, beginning at her legs, Lee felt a slight tremor run through her body. He let go and stood away from her, suddenly sick at the thought he might have waited too long to let her breathe.

Might have killed her.

Then as he watched, staring hard, Lee saw the girl's chest heave and heard her gasp in a long, long breath. She moaned, her head thrown back, and Lee saw her eyes slowly to come to life again.

Not dead then, and not going to die.

Out of what well-spring of desire, Lee didn't know, since he'd damn near scared himself with the trick as much as he had the girl, but Lee found that his cock was swollen to bursting, lay caught in his trouser crotch like a hot iron bar as he stood above the gasping girl.

Damn the little bitch and her promises!

He reached down, slid his hands up under her skirt, along the long soft, solid muscles of her thighs —found the lace and ruffles of her underdrawers, gathered that in his hand, and began to tug them down her legs.

The girl stirred, still gasping for breath, trying feebly to push him away, but Lee yanked the underwear down her long stockinged legs, tore the flimsy material over her red high-heeled shoes and tossed it to the floor.

The odor of her came up to him, rich, warm, sweet and sweaty, with a darker smell. Lee flipped her short skirt up and out of his way, put his hands on her smooth, naked strong-muscled thighs, and pulled them wide apart. She struggled slightly, her head still thrown back into the settee's cushions as she caught her breath, recovering from her faint.

He forced her spraddled thighs wide, straining the large tendon that ran along the inside of each leg, and up into her groin. Stretched her naked and wide, and stood staring down at her.

She was one of the hairy ones—the join of her crotch, the puffed softness of her cunt (divided by a narrow wrinkled slice of pink) and the twin white rounds of her ass were all fuzzed over with delicate little curls of dark blond hair as soft as the fur of a cat.

Lee slid his hands up higher, into those fine curls and warmth and dampness, and pulled her privacies apart and wide open. The small cunt gaping like a nestling's mouth—wet and pink, stretched wide in its frame of fur; her asshole, tiny, brown and round, stretched open, too, to its smaller circumference. The curls of hair grew like soft golden grass right up the long curved crack of her ass.

Lee slid a finger up into her cunt, then forced in another.

The girl moaned, struggled, and tried to sit up. Lee shoved her roughly down again, his hand working at her, fingers exploring up into the wet and heat of her. She kicked weakly out at him, and Lee pinned that leg wide with his knee, and began to unbotton his trouser flies with one hand, while his other hand was at her like some powerful, curious little animal—spreading, probing, searching up into her, his fingers wet and sticky with her juices.

Lee got his trousers and underdrawers open, and then his cock was out, throbbing, swollen, hard as seasoned wood.

He heard another sound, then—turned his head, startled—and saw a figure at the canvas curtains at the back of the box.

It was the ticket girl—the one who'd come before with the actress's fake call from "Mister Hawkins." The stocky girl stood still, staring at Lee, the swollen cock jutting from his trousers, and at the actress's sprawled legs, her naked thighs, her cunt stretched wide by Lee's wet, glistening fingers.

For an instant, blinded by his need for the half-naked girl before him, Lee stood frozen, waiting for the other woman to run yelling for help.

But she didn't.

Dim in the near darkness, her white, round face shining softly in the glow of the box's single gas light, the stocky girl only stood and watched. Then she licked her lips. "Jesus . . ." she said, her voice hoarse. "You're doin' it to her, ain't yuh . . ." And stayed where she was just inside the curtain, staring.

Lee's heart was hammering fit to break in his chest. He stroked his cock. "You want some of this, too?"

The girl shook her head, slowly. She was staring at the actress, staring at what Lee's hand was doing. "Go on, then . . ." she said.

"Sally?" the actress said and heaved half up off the sofa. "Help . . ." Lee's free hand clamped tight to her mouth again, forcing her back and down as he leaned in against her and, using his cunt-wet fingers to guide it, set, shoved, and then thrust all the length of his cock up and into her. To the root.

The actress heaved and bucked as he drove it in all the way, thrusting hard with all the muscular power of his hips and thighs to split her, open her up.

He drove for the center, the hot heart of her, as if he were killing her with it.

She screamed against his hand. And the girl by the curtained doorway echoed that muffled cry, staring, her eyes glittering, reflecting the flame of the lamp.

For the first few moments, Lee was lost in the girl, lost to anything else but the squeezing warmth, the slipperyness of her inside.

She grunted into his smothering hand as he bucked against her, thrusting into her with a wet smacking sound. He reached down, hooked his hand behind her knees, and pulled her thighs up and out, shoving her legs back so that her hairy cunt—the hair wet now, sticking in darkened ringlets to his cock as he pulled out of her, rough around the skin of his cock as he drove back in.

Her small cunt was stretched open, gaping, clenched around him as he filled her, shuttling back and forth. He slid a hand down her thigh, found the tiny pucker of her ass and worked his forefinger into her there, screwing it deep into her.

The girl gasped against his hand, shuddered, and as Lee stared near blind with pleasure down into her contorted face, he saw that she was weeping.

"Oh—oh, Jeeesus, but you're givin' it to her . . ." the girl by the curtain said. "Jeeesus—but you're fuckin' her good!" The girl's eyes were on the young actress like a cat's wide in the dimness, as if to see all, everything . . .

Then just by that quick glance up to the watching girl, something seemed to drift across Lee's pleasure . . . his attention.

It was not the first time he'd been with two women—not the first time a second woman had taken pleasure in watching. It was something else.

He looked down at the little actress . . . *Adah.* She lay curled and contorted beneath his weight and strength, covered by the ruffles of her upflung skirt, except where her sprawled thighs left her naked, exposed to him.

Lee suddenly pulled back and free of her with a damp sucking sound and stood unsteady, his cock, wet with her oil, swaying before him.

"Ooooh . . ." The girl by the curtain.

The little actress was weeping like a child, her face turned to the cushions, her slight body shuddering with her sobs.

The girl by the curtains stood watching them both, her eyes wide, unblinking.

"*God damn it to hell!*" Lee ground out the curse and then stood straight, and, not without difficulty, managed to stuff his rod back down into his trousers. The damn thing was still stiff as a post.

The front of his trousers was soaked. He pulled his clawhammer coat closed and buttoned it. Didn't quite hide the wet place, but it helped.

He bent to touch the girl on the shoulder, to draw her skirt down to cover her, but she flinched back with such a look . . . It was a kind of mindless terror he'd seen on some women's faces, a look they had after their pimp had beaten them on the top floor of some rough house. Lee'd seen that look a few times. God-damned if he'd ever thought to *cause* a woman to appear like that!

He felt a flush of shame rising clear up from his boots and had the sudden notion of handing the girl his pistol, or something of that sort, to let her take a revenge on him. He felt like a yellow dog rather than a man.

"Listen," he said to the girl as she lay weeping. "Listen to me, now—you shouldn't work to fool a man that way. You—you don't understand what drives a man that way! You shouldn't fool him . . ."

He bent and searched the dimness of the box for his Stetson, feeling worse and worse as he hunted like a fool until he found it beneath the red settee where one of the actress's stockinged legs still hung limp, as if he'd broken her bones.

He found the hat, jammed it down on his head, painfully near to tears himself, and said, "Please, little lady—please forgive me for what I did. I played the dog, and I bitterly regret it . . .!"

He turned, brushed past the girl at the curtains, and went up to the two steps and out into the corridor, breathing as hard as if he'd run for his life for more than a mile.

Lee stood dazed by the brighter lights in the hall —its white painted wooden walls, a gas lamp every few feet, it seemed like—stood there getting his bearings, then plunged along the narrow passage, heading for the stairway door. There was nothing he wanted so much as a breath of outdoor air. God help the man who tried to stop him!

He got to the door, wrenched it open, and started down the narrow steps with a clatter of boot heels, got to the small, square landing—and stopped.

"*Jesus H. Christ!*" He hadn't paid for that God-damned champagne! And if he knew a flash joint, the owners would take the price out of the girl's salary—or her hide.

Lee groaned . . . hesitated . . . then slowly turned and clumped back up the steps. Would rather take a beating. Would a hell of a lot rather take a beating than go back into that damn velvet theatre box.

He went back up the steps, through the door, and up along the narrow corridor. A couple passed him, there—old folks; looked like some merchant and his wife (God knew what the two of them would think about the goings-on he'd just forced on that girl—*and* that other bitch coming in and staying to see. . . Though, coming to the *Bella Union*, the old folks must have some kind of notion of gay doings).

Lee stopped at the curtains to his box, mighty reluctant to draw them aside. It occured to him and for the first time that maybe these San Franciscans might take a thing like this mighty hard. They appeared to have been more than some taken with

Miss Adah. Might like to hang any fellow that abused her. Be hard to blame them for it, too.

Lee heard some sort of talking . . . murmuring, through the curtains. Likely that damn cat-eyed ticket girl comforting her. No sounds of crying, anyway.

He put his hand on the curtain edge, gently put the material aside, worrying lest his face call forth some damn noisy screaming or other. Would make a hanging more than a notion, for sure, if a fuss brought a crowd . . . .

Lee eased the curtain aside and put his head through slowly already looking like a damn bad boy —and damned sorry for it—to soften the actress up if she started to fuss. He looked in.

And saw, in a rosy gloom, the actress, Adah, still lying as he had left her, stretched sprawled across the little sofa, her skirts flung up, her forearm laid across her eyes. Still weeping, but more softly, sniffling a little. And kneeling before her, crouched between those long, white-thighed, wide-spread legs, murmuring comfort, kissing gently, the stocky little ticket girl. The ticket girl's eyes were closed. Her head moved slowly, left to right, kissing softly . . . kissing gently. She said something quietly, then leaned forward, bent her head and stayed in that attitude for a little while.

The actress moved a little in the velvet cushions, restlessly.

Then—so soft was the sound that Lee had to strain to hear it—he heard a faint, rapid lapping sound. It sounded like a small dog drinking from a bowl of water.

The actress said, "Oh . . . don't . . . " and slowly, slowly raised one knee. And then slowly raised the other, until Lee saw no more of the kneeling girl than her little lace cap. White, round pillars of thigh stood at either side of her head. The little lace cap moved between. The little dog was grunting as it drank.

Slowly, slowly, the actress raised her long legs fully into the air as if she were a flower, and so, in gas light, spread her petals and strained her legs straight up and back, her toes pointed at the ceiling. The little dog sounded starved for what it ate. The actress's legs began to move in the air as if she were dancing, slowly.

Lee stood at the curtains, watching and listening about all that he *could* watch and listen, without jumping on in there to join those ladies. But something told him *better not.* He'd had his chance which had proved not any chance at all, but just some bullying, and would damn sure be unwelcome now.

The ticket girl—a Sapphic, sure—had been her chance and taken it. Caught the girl frightened, outraged . . . exhausted. Kisses, hugs, comforting . . . then this.

Lee watched the little actress begin to writhe with pleasure, her long legs straining up and back as the kneeling girl tended to her, licking, sucking, goggling at her privates, not caring what noises she made. The kneeling girl's face was smeared with wet in golden gas light.

Lee felt sweat start out on his brow as he watched—and then had had enough. It was time to get out or get the hell back in there.

He'd pressed his luck enough.

He stepped quietly back, away from the curtains, and let them fall silently into place. Then he started down the hall. And though his cock felt mighty sorry to be going, Lee himself felt something relieved.

It had been the damndest foolishness . . . had shown him something about himself, too, that maybe he'd rather not have known. The fine Mister Morgan, horse rancher and gentleman, (only not all that much of a gentleman, when you come right down to it). Something of a rough, when you came right down to it—perhaps something of a dog, as well.

And hadn't paid for the damn champagne, after all. Not that that little Adah would be noticing that for a while.

Down the hall to the door, and down the stairs a wiser man, and still sweating his shirt to a rag, Lee bucked a crowd coming into the theatre for the next show (they were missing a hell of a one up in that box) and shouldered his way out into the barroom.

Never was happier to be in a saloon in his life.

He forged ahead on a straight path toward the nearest working barkeep, and paid little heed to the men he jostled aside. The barkeeper watched Lee approach with the eyes of a man who had seen everything there was to see in the face of a man needing a drink as bad as can be. He only lifted an eyebrow when Lee was still twenty-feet from the mahogany —Lee nodded—and the barman turned to pour him a double shot of rye. The fellow knew his business. Lee got to the wood just as the glass of whiskey was set down before him, and settled in snugly between a sport in a busted-back jacket and a squat lumber-jacker who smelled like a bear.

Lee was willing to call that fine company.

CHAPTER EIGHT

A HALF hour later, he was out on the street and standing, the night crowds hurrying past, in a fine sea-smelling, cooling fog, not thick enough to hide the lights and lanterns or to muffle the sounds of music and laughter and trouble all down the neighboring blocks.

Lee'd stopped worrying much about that vigilante hanging party as soon as he'd seen the little actress's legs in the air, that ticket girl down between them. Still, he'd drunk his whiskey and talked axes with the lumberjacker with one eye cocked to the theatre entrance all the while, for a grease-painted crowd out for vengeance.

The *Bella Union* had been all she'd been cracked up to be. And Lee was damned glad to be out of it. He'd gone in there with a better opinion of himself than he carried now, that was for sure. Never had thought of himself as a woman-abuser. Didn't care for the thought of it. His hand over the girl's face . . . using his strength against her as if she were some animal had to be wrestled down and held against its will. . . .

Something to remember, next time he got to feeling better than other men—younger, richer, tougher. Something to remember. If Catherine Dowd could ever somehow come to know of it—just for a for-instance—well, Lee would never be able to see her again. Would never be welcome at Spade Bit again.

A nasty shame to swallow and keep. And not the least of it, leaving her weak and ready for the ticket girl, same as if the Sappho had hired him to cadet the girl for her and he more than willing to do it.

Lee, half hustled along by the sidewalk crowd, began to walk down hill, down toward the waterfront he guessed. The hill was steep enough, he thought, that a drunk might lose his balance, start to roll, and not stop 'till he hit salt water.

Lee got to a corner, turned, and crossed the street. The fog was thick enough now that he couldn't read the street signs. Anyway, he'd forgotten the directions that snotty desk clerk had given him to the place . . . Blackie's . . .

"Say," he said, and as he stepped up onto a boardwalk, caught a passing fellow by the arm. This whole steep street seemed lined with boardwalks—likely the mud or tides or whatever made it too wet for pavement down here. "Say," he said. The man he'd stopped looked scared, 'till he noticed Lee's Stetson—probably'd thought him one of the local hard-cases out to rob him. "What d'yuh want, Mister?" trying to tug away.

"Blackie's," Lee said.

The man waved away, down into the fog, pointing further down the street. "Treat Alley," he said, yanked his jacket sleeve out of Lee's grip, and was gone.

Lee kept on the way he had been and it was like walking down into a dream. Here, on each side of the narrow street, were huddled crowds moving slowly along, faces and hands dead white through the soft, gray haze of fog—the fog pierced, here and there, by the blaze of light from some open doorway, open windows above.

"*Saaay, Jocko!*"

Lee looked up, and saw a woman standing naked at a second story window. Her bare breasts shook as she leaned out over the sill in a flood of red lamp light, calling "Jockoooo!"

A man was shouting across the street. "Here they are! Here they are! Real girly girls . . . real pretty little waitress girls! You want—they do!" He had a deep, rolling bass voice that boomed through the mist, the darkness and light like a war drum. Lee looked across the street but couldn't make the man out amidst the shuttling glare and shadows, the passing crowd—silent, or yelping drunk.

"*Little waitress girls! You want—they do. Two bits to look—three bits to touch—four bits for everything! Real soft girly girls!*"

Lee saw an alley mouth and ducked into it, glad to be out of the crowd for a moment. Having all those people around him, not being able to see them well in the fog, made him nervous as a young horse.

He didn't know if this was Treat Alley or not, but it was quieter than the street. Odd music coming from the dirt . . . Then he saw it wasn't from the dirt, but from the cellar stair—a coal chute, it looked like, that someone had put steps into.

Lee walked over to it, glad of his boots in the wet, yielding filth he was stepping in, and peered down into a shaft of soft yellow light. The music had a strident sort of twanging sound. There were strange smells—the oddest mix of perfume and wood smoke and shit stink . . .

It seemed to him this might be some sort of Chinese place, not for whites, and Lee started to run away just as a thin lady in a black dress stuck her head up from the well of light, peered up through the drift of fog, saw Lee looking down and beckoned to him as if he'd been long expected and now was late.

If the woman, who was Chinese, very thin, with a flat, angry, slit-eyed face—if she had stayed in the cellar mouth and argued and cajoled, then Lee would have turned and left. It was peculiar, though, that by beckoning once then sinking away back down into her well of light and noise, she seemed to leave him no option but to follow her.

Lee stooped, found a top step—more a ladder-rung than a step—and carefully climbed down, blinking in the brightness, and warmth, the jangle of music and voices.

He was the only white man there. The whole of the long room—reaching back, he supposed, to the end of the building above it—was packed with Chinese men and women (many more of the men, of course) and all of them packed in around six or seven long tables at which some sort of game seemed to be being played with square white counters.

The men were betting, that was certain, and they were mad with the fever of it. Waiters forced their way through the crowds at the tables, delivering bowls of white worms, it appeared to Lee, which the Chinamen would take, flip a coin to the waiter for, and scoop directly into their mouths with a pair of sticks.

It was the damndest performance Lee had seen, as to eating, and it was a disappointment to him, on looking at and smelling some of the stuff in a bowl a chattering waiter presented to him off of a fine shining black tray, when Lee realized the stuff was boiled dough of some kind, and not worms at all.

Lee had seen the men taken with gambling fever—and watched more than one man ruin himself at Faro, or poker, or on the wheel. He'd seen drunks and hop-heads play for their last pennies—for their horses and saddles, some of them. But he'd never seen men gamble like this.

There was a fever in the place and it raged back and forth across the room as the Chinamen screamed and shouted their bets while the counters clattered and flew like wood chips out from under a steam saw. And all this in a setting painted bright scarlet and gold, reminding Lee uncomfortably of the *Union*, and that damned theatrical box.

Lee felt mighty out of place down here, too, and looked around for the thin woman who had beckoned him in. He'd seen plenty of Chinese, of course, laundrymen and cooks up in Parker, and at some of the ranches. They'd seemed a shy people to him . . . a quiet people. Now Lee realized that that had been company manners he'd seen—the way Chinese behaved in the midst of white strangers.

Here, he was the stranger. And he felt it.

There was a tug at the back of his clawhammer coat, and Lee turned quickly—more than a little jumpy, was the truth (and wondering what in hell he'd followed the woman down for)—to see that lady herself, still gripping the tail of his coat. She let go of it, reached up to grab hold of his sleeve and, saying something he couldn't hear above the gamblers' uproar, pulled him along after her as she shoved and elbowed her way through the crowd toward the back of the basement.

It was go along or cut and run for the steps. Lee couldn't bring himself to break and run—he could imagine only too clearly what he'd look like, a well-dressed white rancher, likely armed (as indeed he was), twice the size of any other man present, a white man in a white man's country, running like a scalded cat to claw his way up those steps and out.

He preferred not to provide that sort of entertainment for a bunch of gaming orientals.

So he followed the thin woman as she hauled him along and noticed that none of the Chinese people seemed to see him as he strode past them. They crowded in on every side, talking, laughing, shouting with excitement around the big tables, eating strings of white dough from little shining bowls, and a few, not many, sitting on benches along the wall, listening to three men playing at stringed instruments of some kind.

San Francisco appeared to be a very musical city. Even the Chinese apparently needed to have an instrument band of their own odd sort playing to entertain them, no matter how hard it was to hear the music above the uproar of the gamesters.

And still all down the length of this smoky and noisy cellar not one Chinese met Lee's eyes, or had since he'd come in, except for the woman who led him through them now and the waiter who'd tried to serve him food.

It was like being a ghost—a large, well-dressed white ghost in a wide-brimmed hat.

The thin woman tugged at his sleeve to hurry him up and Lee saw that they were at the room's far end, and before a red and gold-gilt door with a lit paper lantern hanging beside it. The lantern's shade showed a bright red fish swimming in dark blue water.

The woman opened the door and pulled Lee through after her. They were in a corridor then—nearly dark. And quiet. The door closing behind them had shut off the sounds of shouting, the rattle and clatter of game counters, as if it had been a brick wall.

It occured to Lee that a neat knife stuck in his back here in this near dark would leave the lucky Chinaman who wielded it more than two hundred dollars to the good. Lee stooped quickly as the Chinese woman tripped along before him—found the handle of his heavy two-edged dagger at the top of his right boot, drew it, and carefully slid the broad blade up into his left sleeve, grip down, ready for a quick right-handed reach.

He also glanced behind him and saw nothing but bare walls . . . shadows.

The thin woman stopped suddenly, and Lee walked full tilt into her, stepped back, and excused himself as if she were a lady. The Chinese woman paid that no mind, grunted with some sudden exertion of effort, and swung a wide door open on groaning hinges.

The sudden light made Lee blink. Then he saw the thin woman take several steps into a long room almost as big as the cellar room they'd left, turn to him, and make a sort of elegant, presenting gesture about her. As if offering him a very great deal indeed.

And so she was.

Ranged along both walls and extending at least sixty or seventy feet to the back were a row of tiny cubicles, little closet rooms, each no more than four feet across, no more than eight feet deep. These closets were made of wood framing and open wire mesh, and a second row was stacked like shipping crates on top of the bottom one.

In each of these cribs that Lee could see—thirty to forty of them, for sure—a young oriental girl sat, naked except for a short red silk shirt.

They were, most of them, at their ease, chatting in their language with their neighbors, paying no attention to the wire mesh between them. A few were playing instruments like the ones making a racket back in the cellar room; a few others lay asleep on narrow cots, or lay smoking long-stemmed pipes, holding little smoking wads in the bowls with thin, flat sticks.

It was, with their noise and music and the bright colors of their shirts, much like those cages of birds which Lee had heard of rich people in New York City keeping in their mansions. Cages of birds that reached to high ceilings, filled with color and song.

The Chinese woman tugged at his sleeve again.

"You go in. You do what want, but no break bone, no squeeze throat, no kill." She held out a slender hand. "Two dollah," she said. "Do what want." She gave him a quick, calculating look. "One gal. Two gal, *three* dollah."

Now all the women were looking at him, excepting those still asleep.

This was, Lee supposed, most men's dream—near half a hundred odd and foreign women bare-ass naked and his to have, at least for the moment. Likely there'd soon be other customers led down the corridor as the night rolled on. Most men's dream—but Lee found it unnerving, being stared at by bright black eyes, row on row of them.

Some of the women were pretty things, though. (Two could play the gazing game.) Some of them pretty and damn young, too. There were some no more than kids among them—nine or ten years old, some of them . . .

"Two dollah!" The thin woman made a little snapping motion with her fingers.

Lee sighed, and dug into his trousers for the two bucks.

* * *

It had been one thing to have lounged in a whore house parlor, chatted with the girls, chatted more with your favorite, then, after a drink or two, follow her on upstairs into some privacy . . .

That had been one thing.

This was another.

Near fifty pairs of bright black eyes followed Lee as he strolled, doing his damndest to seem at ease, along that narrow corridor of cages. He saw that the wire screen doors weren't locked in any way. The girls had at least that indication of freedom, however grim the reality. No locks, and little toys and tassled statues. The advantages, it appeared, to being a Chinese whore.

As he paced along, the girls came to the front of their cages, and presented themselves to him, quickly lifting short silk shirts to show small, delicate breasts, as toast-colored as the rest of their slight bodies.

They seemed very clean—no odor to them at all, except for a sort of sweet muskiness, which Lee thought their natural one. And now, looking so closely at them, Lee could see that the girls were each as various in their faces and figures as any group of white girls would have been. Some were thin-faced, harsh and desperate looking; others as soft-cheeked, plump, and merry as any white farm girl might be. The children, though, looked terribly sad . . .

No wonder about that. Eight, nine, ten years old. One little girl, thin as a rail, no more than nine, said, "Look me, sailor!" stood at her mesh door, spread thin thighs, and stuck a finger into her little hairless sex, and wiggled it. "Look me, sailor!"

Lee was beginning to wish his two dollars back in his pocket.

The other women watched him walk. Didn't seem to blink, staring at him. And each one came to her cage door as he passed, some pursing their lips to chirp at him like birds, some calling "Two bits again —and I do you anything!" None of these women, Lee saw, had much hair down there. And all of them were built there as all women were, their small bare slits resting up and down, and not across as some saloon sages had them.

Then, almost at the end of the room, Lee saw a girl sitting on her cot seeming to pay him no mind as he came along. Just above her, in a cage with a short ladder before it, a small fat girl leaned down and called, "Oh, Yankee—Oh, Yankee! You pee-pee here, you like!" and gestured to her open mouth.

But the girl below her called not a word, only sat on her narrow cot and watched Lee come to her cage door as a touchy watch dog might.

She was a medium-sized girl, stronger looking than most of them seemed. Not pretty as some of them, either. She had a flat oriental nose, narrow black eyes, and eyebrows so marked that they looked to have been brushed with charcoal black. Strong looking legs, with calves like a boy's.

Lee stopped by her crib door, perhaps because looking so sullen, so little eager to please, she seemed more human, more of a real girl than did the other chirping, calling, whistling women.

He stopped there and stood and watched her.

She stared at him for a moment, turned her head and leaned over to spit into a chamber pot, then stood up and came to the door mesh and stared back at him, her neck craned because of his height, her eyes as shiny, deep, and cold as the waters of a winter lake.

She was close enough for Lee to smell the faint warmth of her breath.

He smiled down at her, but that made no difference in her expression at all. The same still, gleaming, pitch-black look. The other women were continuing to make their noises . . . shouting.

With no change of expression, the girl suddenly reached down for the hem of her red shirt, lifted the material, pulled the shirt off, and tossed it onto her cot.

Then, as still-faced as ever, she began, very slowly, to do a sort of dance. Almost a kind of gymnastic exercise, it seemed to be. At first facing Lee, the girl slowly raised a sturdy light brown leg, and keeping her balance wonderfully, extended it, turning her foot out, so that Lee's gaze seemed naturally to slide up from her toe-pointed foot, past a fine turned ankle . . . up and up the rounded swelling of her calf . . . past the soft hollow at the back of her knee. Then over the taut smoothness, the full fineness of her thigh.

And into the pocket of her groin, as delicately tinted as a pearl's color, where a small, fat, cushioned mound was very lightly furred and split by neat, slightly open lips. Shining pink, and damp.

She showed that to him, and turned on her other

foot while she did, then put both feet down and slowly spread her thighs splittingly wide and so showed him her cunt stretched fully open, like a small, wet, red cup into which anything might be poured, and reach the center of her.

These slow exercises, more difficult than they appeared, had put a slight film of sweat upon her skin and the lamp light in the room played upon that in shades of sun and wheat.

Having shown Lee her center and once more balanced on just one foot, the girl slowly turned half a circle, and revealed a narrow, finely muscled back, cut across in more than a dozen places by bone-white scars a foot and more long—and below that, buttocks as full, hard, and firm as an acrobat's.

She raised both arms high over her head, her beaten back still to him, then, in the same slow rhythm in which she had done everything, reached down and back with both hands to grip her buttock cheeks, squeezing them in small strong hands so that the fine flesh dented, and then slowly, firmly pulled them wide apart and bent forward. Her anus was a puckered notch, pink and tiny, its small mouth slightly sprung by her stretching grip.

She bent further, quickly, and so displayed to Lee her neat cunt, now closed as a pink-lipped purse, tucked deep up into the closure of her thighs.

Then she stood erect again, the white lines of whipping laced across her small, muscled back, the narrow nape of her neck surprisingly frail under a coiled, drawn-up mass of hair as black as rained-on coal.

Lee—who had had, as she postured, a cock-stand

so rigid that it hurt him, now found himself staring hardest at those whip marks. He had seen the marks of beatings on many whores and some whores were proud of the attention by their macks that such marks represented. But nothing like this. Here, on that small, sturdy, lovely back, the whip had barked like a savage dog, then bitten to her bone.

Finished with her posturing, never having said a word, the Chinese girl turned round again and faced him, as expressionless, as hard-eyed as before. The top of her head was only slightly higher than his heart.

If Lee had not been slightly drunk, he would never have done it. Would certainly not have done it if he hadn't used the actress girl so roughly at the *Bella Union*. This girl was no common whore and neither were the others. Lee had heard of it, and seeing them here like birds in cages, was quite sure. These were slaves. Bought and sold, and no nonsense about it.

This one, this stern little slant-eyes standing naked in front of him, having shown him all her pretty secrets, having shown him the marks of the whip—this one must be something brave.

Lee, with great regret, whistled good-bye to his hard-on, turned away from the girl's cage and saw the thin woman just coming in the door again—and behind her four boys, white (and noisy drunk) and not one of them more than a kid.

Lee waited until the woman had collected her dollars—waited 'till the boys, giggling, shouting advice to one another, were started down the row of women—then beckoned the thin woman over. She looked surprised to find him still dressed and not mounted on one of her objects. When she came over, Lee saw a quick savage glance directed at the silent girl—as if, from this one, some difficulty was an old story.

"How much?" Lee said, indicating the girl with his thumb. The girl said nothing, and did nothing. She just stood there.

"For two dollah—what you like!" looking puzzled. "You make bleed—moh dollah!"

"To buy."

"Huh?"

"To buy. *Purchase.*"

The thin woman seemed astonished. Lee wondered how he'd ever thought the Chinese expressionless; she opened her eyes in comic surprise, puffed out her cheeks, and turning, called something in Chinese to the caged woman nearby. The women chittered in astonishment, screeched and laughed, and made mournful faces of pity at Lee.

"Funny," the thin woman said, and nodded, smiling. "You funny."

"I mean it."

At this, the Chinese woman gave him another, more careful look, judging with years of experience of men of all colors and kinds, in all conditions of sobriety, drunkeness, sense and foolishness. She studied him, and then looked at the girl, pursing her lips, considering.

Then, "two hunderd fifty dollah," she said, dead serious. And watched him carefully, watching his eyes in the damp light.

It was within fifty dollars of all that Lee had earned in driving, fighting, and killing for the herd over the past weeks. And that for a furious little yellow slut who had performed whatever men required of her, likely since she was eight years old. And when she balked at this extreme or that had been whipped half to death for it.

A toilet for years—she looked near sixteen now—for the grossest whims of men. And scarred like a galley slave in the bargain.

"Done," Lee said to the thin woman, and held out his hand.

She hesitated, surprised, then put her hand out as well. Lee noticed how fine that hand was, slender and nervous; it occured to him that this thin, plain Chinese woman might herself be a whaler in bed. It was an odd thought, and maybe she caught it, because she glanced up at him and made an odd face.

"Deal," she said.

Lee dug out his purse, and amidst a soprano chorus of startlement and surprise from all that room full of women (except for the silent girl herself, who seemed to be paying no attention to what was happening) he counted out and paid over two hundred and fifty dollars in gold, feeling with every coin like a greater and greater jackass. He and his friends had always had their fun with young boys, drovers and laborers, who, astonished by the nearness and nakedness of whores, immediately fell in love and foolishness with them. That was a whore house commonplace, and a running joke to see enacted.

Well, here he was, making those foolish boys look

like justices of the U.S. Supreme Court by comparison. And not even the excuse of being dead drunk.

The girl, of course, would scoot away, wander for a time, and then, no doubt, return to the only home . . . the only place she knew.

It was money thrown away. It was a great deal of money thrown away. And Lee got his first jibe double quick.

"Sweet Jesus—this rube just *bought* one!" It was one of the four boys, a short, tough-looking kid with sandy hair and a tweed cloth cap. The boy had called back to the others. Two of them were standing watching the third in one of the cages, a thin boy with long white skinned legs, standing naked, his trousers down to his ankles, while a Chinese girl about nine years old knelt before him, mouth stretched wide, face distorted, sucking at his cock with slow tugging movements of her small head.

This, for everyone to watch.

"Say, hick!" the sandy-haired boy said. "You bought the wrong one. You got to get that one held down, you want to screw her in the ass." He was a bright looking boy, pleasant faced and tough.

One of the boys watching the thin boy being serviced, looked back at that and laughed.

"It's a difficulty you won't have to worry about any more," Lee said, "Big-city." And stepped up to the kid with one long stride and kicked him in the nuts. The toe of the cowboy boot caught the boy just right—Lee felt one of the kid's oysters break at the blow.

The sandy-haired boy bent swiftly at the waist and fell sideways to the floor, knotted and grunting with pain.

"Saaay—you son-of-a-bitch!" One of the others spun away from what he'd been watching, yanked a bright thing of brass out of his jacket pocket and ran at Lee, slipping the brass knuckles over his right fist as he came. "He ball-kicked London!"

"What . . . ?" said the one standing in front of the kneeling child. He sounded dreamy with pleasure as the little girl licked and suckled at him.

"He put Jack down!" The third boy came running up behind his brass-knuckled friend—he came bare-fisted.

The room was dead silent. The forty or more women all turned to plaster statues with gleaming, hooded eyes.

The first kid, with the knuckles on, reached Lee, set himself, and swung as Lee ducked and dodged away.

There were too many to fool with. Three tough boys on their feet were three too many. Lee had no notion of being beaten broken-boned.

Stepping back fast as the boy, his friend beside him now, came after him again, Lee reached back and under the right tail of his coat and after an instant's fumbling, drew the Bisley Colt's.

The sight of it—the neat slight sound of the hammer going back to cock—stopped the boys still.

Lee saw then the second boy had an opened Barlow knife in his left hand.

"Drop your usefuls and get on to the back of this room, or I'll kill you."

Lee was surprised to hear himself say that—about killing them. He had intended no such thing, had not intended to say it, anyhow. But he had said it, and realized he'd meant it.

The two boys looked into his face . . . his eyes, for a moment. Then the one with the brass knuckles slipped them off his fist—he was a short, thick-shouldered kid, no more than sixteen or seventeen years old. He had eyes as dark as a Jew's.

"Put it down," this boy said to his friend, who still held the Barlow knife, and his friend, an odd looking kid with teeth like a rabbit's, obediently let it fall clattering to the floor.

"Come on," Brass-knuckles said, and turned away from Lee and the other boy down to the end of the room. From their cages, the women watched, but made no sound at all.

Lee thought that Brass-knuckles showed some promise—a longer head than most toughs his age. The tall kid still standing with his pants down before the little girl, had turned his head to watch the scramble but hadn't moved otherwise.

Lee strode down the aisle of cages to that cage, pulled the mesh door open, stepped in and as the boy, jaw gaping, tried to stumble away, his trousers still caught around his ankles, Lee swung the Colt's full-arm and struck the boy in the mouth with the barrel and broke his teeth.

The boy, still half-naked, fell into the mesh and to the floor, kicking like a shot buck.

The little girl stayed kneeling, staring up at Lee, mouth wet, eyes wide with fear.

Lee couldn't bear to look at her.

He turned, shoved his way out of the cage again and saw the thin Chinese woman standing beside the door to the damn place. Two Chinese men stood with her. They didn't seem impressed by the Colt's in Lee's hand. Not afraid at all. They stood, in long black dresses and black slouch hats, and looked him in the eye as cool as iced fruit salad.

One, the one on the left, was holding a bright-headed hatchet in one hand; the other, a parrot-grip Colt's .38.

This would be killing trouble.

Lee rode his temper as if it were a wild stallion. He hauled in on the curb with all he had.

"You bony bitch," he called to the thin woman, "how much trouble do you want?" It would have to be the man with the pistol first, then the one with the hatchet, if that man only gave him the time . . . was not too quick.

Then the woman. If there was time. The woman, too.

She was a very clever woman and had seen about as much of men as there was to see. Perhaps she saw some shadow of her death in Lee's eyes . . . perhaps, a daughter of an ancestor-worshipping people, she even saw the shadow of someone else in Lee's eyes.

"I not so foolish," she called, reached out, and put her elegant, long-fingered hands, restraining, on the sleeves of the two armed men.

What then, in Lee's heart, felt so like disappointment?

CHAPTER NINE

IT WAS going to cost him even more.

What a damned fool! If it got out, he might as well stay in San Francisco—there'd be no going back to the range. The smiles would never cease.

The wait while the scar-backed girl, his bought girl, had gathered a little bundle of things, a small lamp shade, a little brass statue of a smiling woman, a red pillow—had gathered this trash up and tied it together, had put on a pair of black pyjamas and a ragged black man's hat, all tugged out from under her cot . . .

The wait for her to get that done—then the long walk down the corridor and into the gambling den and through that crowd, the girl trailing behind him, the mob of Chinese stopping their play (likely for the first time since any had shipped into the city) and staring like snakes at Lee leading the girl out and up the ladder of steps to the alley and darkness, fog, coolness, and night; it was a stroll Lee would have been pleased to deny himself.

And now, out in the alley, Lee had seen that the little slave girl—so hard, so stony brave in her brothel—was terrified by the bustling, foggy, lamplit streets, the crowds of whites trampling by, their white faces and white hands just visible through the sea mists rolling up from the bay.

She must have hardly been allowed out of doors at all, and then only in some guarded convoy of wagons to rumble down the street to "air the goods."

The slave pens had been her life, Lee supposed, for almost all of her fifteen or sixteen years. She was as helpless as a baby out of that den of cages.

"You speak any English?"

Silence. A trace of tears in those coal dark eyes. Been a long time, likely, since those eyes had wept.

He'd been a God-damned fool and it was going to cost him even more money. (The lost two-hundred and fifty dollars didn't bear thinking about.) Now it was going to cost him five bucks more.

Lee dug down in his pockets for greenbacks, unfolded the wad, peeled off five single dollar bills and handed them to her.

She stood in the shadows, her hand held out, the five dollars clutched tight, and stared up at him. Lee looked back, and had a thought. There had to be some sort of rescue society, some minister or churchman do-gooding in the city—there always were. Salvation Army, that sort of thing.

"You know Salvation Army?"

Not a twitch. She still stood staring up at him, the dollar bills sticking out of her closed hand.

"Do you know the way to the *Palace Hotel? The Palace?*"

She looked up at him as if she were certain he would learn Chinese in just a minute or two.

He'd wanted to send the sad little whore on her way or at least let her go wait in the *Palace* stables 'till he could rope some Christer in to take her off his hands.

No such luck.

And god-damned if he intended to lose a night's pleasure just to herd her back to the Palace or to some church-house either.

Let her trail or let her wander. She had the damn five dollars and had cost him a lot more. And no fuck for it, either!

Lee patted the girl on the shoulder, said, "You ask Chinese person for the Salvation Army," illustrating "Chinese" by putting his fingers up to his eyes and pulling them aslant. Then he smiled at her, turned, and walked away.

A few feet down the boardwalk, he turned around. As near as he could tell through the fog, she wasn't following. With considerable relief, he walked on, wondering if he should keep looking for Treat Alley, and this *Blackie's,* or give it to go-by and try somewhere else. Damned if he was ready to crawl back to his hotel and call it a night!

Halfway down the block opposite a really noisy dance hall (stomping, romping boots—music like a military band gone mad) Lee stopped to look back. No sign of her, thank God . . .

He walked on a few more steps, said "God damn it to hell!" loud enough so that two men passing stepped away from him without breaking stride and then turned around and marched back up the boardwalk.

At first he didn't see her, and was something relieved.

Then he did.

She was right where he'd left her, but crouching down, huddling against the smoke stained brick there as if that wall was her only friend in the world.

She heard his footsteps and turned to look, her face a mask of tragedy. Lee stood and stared down at her for a moment.

"Oh, there now . . ." he said, "now, now, honey," and she flew into his arms like a bird.

In a box—and the lid nailed down.

"We don't have any Chinks in here, cowpoker. They ain't allowed in here any way at all."

This greeter . . . bouncer, whatever, was about the biggest man Lee'd seen. Even bigger than the Iroquois had been, and odd looking in the bargain. Lumpy looking, with a massive outsize jaw, forehead on him like an ape's, and huge bony knuckles near big as baseballs.

Misshapen is what the fellow was, and just about seven feet all, Lee thought. Must weight three hundred, three-fifty. Not young, either, some gray in that scant hair, stringy mustache . . .

"She doesn't have to go inside your place," Lee said, trying to stay friendly. He had found Blackie's, after all. On *Tritt* alley, not "Treat," and right down on the corner of the street. Lee'd seen ship's masts and rigging through the fog down here.

The place from what he could see in the narrow entrance hall looked mighty fancy. There was a piano and a violin playing together inside.

"Don't make no nevermind, she ain't even comin' in the door." The huge man grinned. "She ain't even stayin' on them *steps*, Sport."

"You have a coat room in there, don't you? She can sit in there and wait for me, damnit!" It was getting harder for Lee to keep his temper.

"Now, be reasonable," the big man said, staying gentle in a professional way. "You wouldn't want to come to no joint that let niggers in, would you?" He looked down at Lee, the Chinese girl ghosting behind him. "Nothin' personal, Sport. But we don't allow no Chinks in Black Jack's place. No how."

Lee was tired of running out of places all over the city.

"You get out of my way, big fellow," he said. "Or I'll *put* you out of my way."

The huge man's small brown eyes widened a little at this. Then he smiled and seemed to relax his shoulders in the tent cloth drape of his fine black coat. His hands, big as spade blades, seemed to grow bigger. "Don't be foolish," he said.

Lee's hand was starting back under the tail of his clawhammer coat when an amused voice said, "*And that would certainly be foolishness. I'd reconsider, if I were you.*"

A man stepped out from beside the giant, and smiled at Lee in a friendly way. As the giant had been the biggest man Lee had seen, so this fellow appeared to be the handsomest. He was an extraordinarily fine looking fellow. Big, easily Lee's height, and a little heavier, the man looked like a sleek, powerful tom cat, with a tom cat's blunt, handsome face. His hair was black and swept straight back, and he wore a narrow, cropped mustache. Eyes, a cool considering gray, and skin as white as a girl's.

Must be catnip to the ladies, Lee supposed, though the fellow's ears did stick out some—a San Francisco fault, apparently. Man was dressed to the nines, too, in a fine black broadcloth suit, snow-white shirt, and black pearl studs.

A fancy fellow, and no mistake. *Blackie,* in the flesh, Lee thought.

And was right.

"Wants to bring in that Chink twist, Blackie. I told him no dice."

The handsome man stepped to one side to get a better look at the girl trying to stay hidden behind Lee. Then, "My, my . . ." he said. "She's a slave, isn't she?"

"Was." Lee said.

"*Was,* huh?" The handsome man smiled, showing even teeth, as white as his shirt. "Where'd you get her?"

"Up the street."

Blackie and the giant exchanged a look. "Up at T'ien's?"

"I wouldn't know her name."

The handsome man threw back his head and laughed. "Moose," he said to the giant, "our young friend here has bought a girl off T'ien—and kept her, so far." He smiled at Lee. "That Chinese lady I'm talking about doesn't let her goods slip, you know what I mean? No matter what you paid."

"She didn't try and stop me; she just took the money."

The handsome man and his giant stood looking at Lee as if he were an odd-man in a raree show. Then the handsome man shook his head and sighed. "I guess we better let the girl in, Moose; she's got this far. Take her back to the kitchen, tell 'em to keep her there."

The giant looked surprised, but nodded and turned away, lumbering down the passage like a draft horse.

Lee took the Chinese girl's shoulders and gently pushed her after the big man, nodding and smiling to show it was all right to go. She took a few steps, then came trotting back to him.

The handsome man, watching this charade, laughed and said a few words to the girl in Chinese. She shook her head and he said something more. Then she gave Lee a last look, turned, and went after the giant, easy as a puppy.

"Where'd you learn to speak that?" Lee said when the girl was gone.

"You spend your life on the Coast, you learn a lot of lingos—at least some bits of them," Blackie said. "I do business with those people from time to time . . ." He looked Lee up and down. "Now, cowboy, what's your pleasure?"

"Some gambling," Lee said. "Some dancing, and the use of a lady.'

Blackie smiled. "No beefsteak dinner?"

"I've had my dinner."

"Then come on in, and take what you can—and don't cry if you lose right after." He led the way down the hall, pushed open a pair of double doors, and preceded Lee into a blaze of lamplight and music.

The place was small compared to the *Bella Union*, no bigger than an ordinary fine saloon. But this room was choice. It was decorated in gray and gold, and a big crystal chandelier, as fine as any such thing Lee'd seen, hung at the center of the room.

The place was crowded, people packed around tables framing a small dance floor—jammed now, with couples dancing a fast, butt-shaking quick-step. Four fiddles, a drum, and the piano were tearing out the music as fast as bows and fingers could fly from a small orchestra stand in the back of the room. The place was thundering, shaking from the dancing.

"Never saw the hootchie-cootchie?" Blackie asked him.

"Not 'till now." It was a dance that looked more like fast screwing than anything else. The women were humping their asses in a whirl of dress fringe and black-stockinged legs. Some of the men looked to be having a hard time keeping up.

"Enjoy yourself, cowboy," the handsome man said and strolled away.

Lee looked longingly at the dancing. It looked prime fun. He noticed the waitresses, too. They bounced about the room with loaded trays of beers and booze, their breasts naked, wearing short skirts, stockings and high-heeled shoes. They seemed not to care where men put their hands while they served out the drinks.

One of these girls spotted Lee standing and cut right over to him, her small breasts trembling as she walked. She was something to see, for she was tattoed like a sailor, with anchors and signal flags and fishes inked in blue into the white of her skin. At each breast, a fish swam with its mouth open, about to swallow a nipple.

Something to see.

She stood in front of him, smiling, letting him look. "Like that?" she said. "That a billy in your pocket, or are you just glad to see me?" She was a merry looking, skinny girl.

Lee laughed, and she motioned with her head to follow and led the way to a small table still covered with spilled beer and the remains of some sandwiches.

The waitress swabbed the table down with a rag she'd tugged from her belt, her breasts shaking briskly in Lee's face. "What'll it be, Handsome?"

"Beer, and a double of rye."

"O.K.," she said, and reached under the table with her right hand to stroke his groin. She felt the bulge of his cock and squeezed it, then straightened up, winked and was gone, threading through the crowd.

It appeared that *Blackie's* was a lively place.

Very lively. At the table next to him, on the right, Lee noticed a pretty girl sitting with another, not so pretty. They were giggling to beat the band and seemed considerable drunk.

Lee looked—then looked again. The not-so-pretty

girl had the makings of a fair growth of beard under her powder. The pretty one, who made a sweet eye at Lee as he looked, had something more muscle in the upper arm than usual in ladies.

The not-so-pretty one leaned over to Lee, having noticed the looks exchanged. "Not looking for trouble, are we, charming boy?" The voice was a warm contralto.

"No," Lee said, "just admiring your taste." The not-so-pretty one blushed with pleasure. "Nicely said," he said, and gave Lee a lingering look himself, so that his friend pouted and reached across their table to rap his knuckles with a fan.

There was some distraction then. A tall man was making a fuss across the room. Had one of the waitress-girls by the arm and was standing up, shaking her. "Fucking thief!" Lee heard over the general merry uproar.

For only a few moments, the tall man stood shouting—then, as Lee watched, two of the fiddlers on the bandstand put their instruments carefully down, picked up baseball bats resting by their music stands, swung over the bandstand railing, shoved through the tables to the scene of the fuss, and appeared to beat the man to death.

The fellow was struck in the head at least twice, with full-armed swings of the bats. Lee heard the solid smacking sounds from where he sat—saw blood fly out to spatter on a table cloth. The man went down and stayed down.

Only a few of the customers seemed interested in that enough to watch it. None of the dancers broke a step.

Lee watched the fiddlers drag the man out through the back. He appeared to slide easily along the polished floor, and left a bright trail of blood behind his head as he went, that a waitress-girl instantly attacked with a mop.

The whole affair from trouble to the end of it had taken perhaps a minute—or two, at most.

A lively place, certainly.

Lee, an hour and several drinks later, felt not the least the worse for wear. He had stood up twice, asked a pleasant girl—a store clerk out with her boyfriend (who was no store clerk)—to dance, and had gotten an exhilarating lesson in the quick-step, slide, and the hootchie-chootchie.

Lee was feeling rosy. He'd had a series of amusing chats with the sissies sitting at the next table, one a city fireman, the other the son of a prosperous ship's chandler. Those two had been full of the gossip of the city. Lee felt he now knew a passel about this big town on the bay, and had also been advised what other sights to see, Telegraph Hill and Seal Rock among them. Had been regaled, as well, with the histories of most of the greatest swells in the city—a terrific series of dizzy climbs out of mining pits, whore houses, dry goods stores and various criminal gangs. The climbers were now, of course, the finest of the fine, tremendously rich and grand.

"Our Blackie, now," the not-so-pretty one had said, nodding in the direction of the proprietor as that fine looking man stopped across the room to speak with an elderly man in elegant evening clothes—"our Blackie, now, is the real article. Dad a

'Sydney Duck,' Mummie a down dock-side whore. He's Coast from way back, and a better fellow you won't find. Game, too—as a fighting chicken," the not-so-pretty one added.

"He's a darling," the pretty one said.

"No chance for you, Sweet-cakes," said her friend.

Lee had bought a round for the sissies in return for the wine they'd bought him, had wished them a friendly farewell (the fireman had duty at the station by four) and was deciding now to try and buck the wheel while he will had a few dollars left to fly with.

He noticed Blackie watching him from across the room, waved to him, and received a nod in return. Was about to get up and go to the roulette against the far wall of the place, when he felt a hand plucking in his coat tail. Lee turned, expecting the Chinese girl to have come out of the kitchen and be bothering him.

It wasn't the Chinese girl.

It was the girl with one blind eye—milky white, that blind eye was—the little whore whose table he'd passed walking through the *Bella Union.* It seemed to have happened a long time ago. She'd had a mack with her then, Lee recalled. A handsome boy with a razor.

"Say, Flashy," the whore said, winking her blind eye, and drawling her words out as many people in the gay life did, "I thought you might be goin' with them two Nancies just left. You a queer one?"

Lee looked behind her. The handsome blue-eyed mack was standing, leaning against the bandstand rail just by the piano. He grinned a business grin at Lee.

"No, I'm not," Lee said, and the girl sat down at his table.

"How'd you like to prove it?" she said.

Lee finished his beer and waited for her pitch.

She was a nice looking girl, with curly brown hair and a snub nose. She didn't look particularly the whore, except for the way she was dressed. And the blind eye.

"I'll do anything you want, Mister," she said, sounding like a Harvey girl about to read off a menu.

"You like a Frenching? I'll suck it an' swallow it for you like buttermilk." She was smiling. "I'll lick your ass for you, too. I like to do that."

She waited to see if he had anything to say to that.

"Or are you only a straight-fucker? Is that what you like? What me to tell how I got my first dickin'? You like that?" She showed him her tongue. "I was ten when my daddy made me do everythin' for him an' his friends. Want me to tell you about that?" She leaned back and said "How's about a beer, Sport, while you make up your mind?"

Lee caught the eye of his waitress, and tipped up his hand twice, for two beers.

"You ever seen a lady do a dog? I'll do that, an' you can watch, an' nobody'll ever know . . ." She sat back and looked at him, and Lee noticed that there was a faint blue ghost of a pupil in the center of her blind white left eye. She seemed to be considering him. "I'll even do a nigger for you—what about that? Like that? See me with a big black nigger?"

Lee saw that the trot had taken him for a rube, pure and simple. He'd noticed that his Stetson and boots provoked that sort of treatment in big towns.

"Tell you what," he said to the one-eyed girl. "I'll go a dollar on a Frenching, here and now." It certainly might be done, and done here and now, since Lee had seen a fat woman fucked by two toughs in a table booth now twenty feet away, and nobody noticing, neither scum nor swells, though they could hardly have missed it, seeing that the woman had squealed loud as Harrigan's pig when she came off.

"Not here," the one-eyed girl said. "Out back."

A badger game, then. They must think he had more money than a simple screwing would get out of him. It appeared to Lee that robbing was the order of the day. Possible, too, they'd heard of the Oakland horse sale; Lee didn't doubt these city toughs had their informants.

Could, of course, tell little One-eye to get lost. And then, sure as sunrise, would meet them in the dark on his way back to the hotel. Could call for Blackie to peel them off his back—could call for some city policemen, come to that, if any patroled the Coast. Lee'd heard the police of this city wore big Bowie knives rather than pistols at their sides. Might be worth seeing if they could use them . . .

No, none of that would do.

The girl and her crimp were here and there was no help for it. And he might get something out of the deal, after all. In any case, he'd already decided.

There'd be no more running out, not tonight. Not from anybody.

"Out back it is," Lee said as the tattooed waitress brought the beers. He paid her, tipped her a dollar, drank his beer down, then watched while the curly-haired whore did the same.

They stood up together. Lee glanced to see the mack, but the blue-eyed man was gone.

The whore led him out through the tables and down a long hall at the back. The hall looked like some part of a gentleman's home—more that than the back corridor of a fancy gambling den with music and dancing and fucking on the side. Lee thought it likely that the owner, Blackie, lived upstairs and had tricked out this hall accordingly. The girl led him past a small staircase on the left, and Lee saw English hunting prints up along the staircase walls and knew he was right.

Not a bad life—to own a place like this—if you kept your nerve facing heavy winners, toughs, trouble, and the law. A fine life, in its way . . . .

Lee watched the girl walk. She walked like a young mare, her neat haunches rising and falling with her stride under the gathered material of her dress. A dasher, and no mistake—and likely a prime ride, when she wasn't out to rob a fellow or have her mack scare him out of his cash. She could learn a thing or two about what clothes to wear—could learn it from those two sissies, come to that. They'd looked more like fine ladies than she did, in that whore-yellow dress with a rope of red feathers around her neck. He wondered how she'd been blinded in that eye . . . Sickness, maybe. More likely a blow, or some other whore sticking a hatpin into it.

The mack would likely be outside . . . would wait a while, 'till his dolly had Lee engaged . . . .

Be a damn shame to be pounded out and wake on a sailing ship heading for God knew where. Would serve him right, being such a fool as to brace this trouble. Could have told the girl he was near broke. Might have believed him. Saved them both, the mack too, considerable trouble.

CHAPTER TEN

THE ONE-EYED girl had been this way before. She reached the end of the hall, opened the door there, stepped up some stairs to the right and pushed open another door, a heavier one. Mist and the smell of the sea came down those steps as Lee went up. The fog had thinned; moonlight silvered the doorway.

He didn't feel drunk; he felt fine.

The girl stood in the dirt of the alley by the open door, waiting for him. Lee stepped out and took her arm like a gentleman, and walked her out into the open to see what the space was like. A back alley, and no mistake. Fifty feet or more long—there appeared to be a pile of garbage at the end of it—and at this end, walled by brick buildings at each side, fenced across by a tall board fence. No more than twelve, fifteen feet wide.

The city must be stringing telegraph stuff down to the docks; there was a huge wooden spool of wire

—some cut-off lengths, a pile of big iron staples and wooden crosstrees. The wire pole was at the far end of the alley; the tar that streaked its sides shone black in the moonlight.

A very likely spot, Lee thought. And doubtless had numerous tales to tell.

"It'll cost you five green for the Frenching, Sport," the One-eyed girl said, pulled a little away from him, and held out her hand. Her white eye shone like a pearl in the moonlight. She was, in a way, a beautiful girl.

Lee had found long since that when trouble was certain sure, it was best to be the one to start it.

He smiled at the girl, reached out with his left hand, and gripped her by the throat. And squeezed.

He might as well have done the same to a big house cat and gotten the same silent strangled explosion of writhing, kicking, and clawing. The girl struck out at him instantly with her nails as if she could tear his throat open with them, kill him. And she kicked for his nuts as swfit and certain as a pool room tough.

Lee turned his hip to avoid the kicks, tightened his grip on her throat (her mouth was stretched wide in a silent scream), heaved her up into the air with that one-handed grip, carried her across the moonlit alley, and slammed her into the board fence. When he let go of her throat, she fell to her knees, heaved in a breath with a whining sound, then started to stand up again, her fingers curled to claws, her small teeth bared as any tigress's. In her swift response, the One-eyed girl told more of her life's story more truthfully than ever she would to get a rise from a customer-John.

Lee glanced around the alley again, saw that the mack had yet to show, and leaned against the struggling girl to press her to the tall fence boards and hold her still. She was just opening her mouth to scream when Lee, stooping slightly, drew the double-edged dagger from his right boot, laid the broad blade flat on her cheek (a broader blade than the toothpick had had, buried with his father) and set the needle point the very slightest bit into her skin, just below the lower lid of her good eye.

"I'll pick it out like an oyster," he said, "unless you're good."

A single drop of blood welled up where the point rested just below her eye.

The nightmare of blindness, which she must have dreamed time after time once her other eye was ruined, closed in upon the girl and broke her. All her fierce spirit fled.

She sank back slowly to her knees in the alley's dirt, and held her head like a crystal thing, balanced upon the needle point of his knife.

Lee stood slowly up, keeping the point of the dagger at her cheek.

"Do what you said you'd do," he said. "Open my trousers, and get to it. And if you touch me with a tooth, I'll have the eye out of your head quicker'n scat."

The girl knelt there, the bright blade across her white cheek, her odd shadow thrown down the length of fencing by the moon, reached out and carefully unbuttoned Lee's trousers, gently reached in and drew him out . . . and carefully, carefully bent her head against the tiny pressure of the knife point to softly kiss, and then begin to lick, the swelling head of his cock as the length of it stiffened in her hands.

This girl had an artist's hands, an artist's mouth for the pleasuring of a man's parts. As Lee slowly eased the pressure of the blade against her cheek she moved her mouth more freely over him, her eyes tight shut (either to try and guard them from the knife, or to concentrate upon her licking and kissing and suckling). Swiftly, whatever her fear, her mouth grew wet and juicy with saliva as she sucked, so that her lips, moving steadily back and forth, stretched wide in an aching "O" to occommodate him, made all the soaked and liquid sounds of the wettest fuck.

As Lee gave a little at the knees with the pleasure of her doing, throwing his meat deeper into her mouth as she worked upon it, the girl began to make a sound in her throat—of passion, perhaps, whores being partial to forcing of one sort or another; perhaps simply as a way to keep from choking.

Her head moved faster there at Lee's crotch; she snorted air through her nostrils as she labored at him, sucking hollow-cheeked as if by sucking hard enough she might have some sort of a revenge.

Lee leaned into her harder, and felt himself begin to suffer a greater and greater pleasure. His balls seemed to knot themselves into a sweet and growing heat. His belly hurt him with the feeling. He gritted his teeth and stared down at her as she tugged at him, her mouth distended, his cock a massive swelling in her cheek. The knife blade lay against that.

Lee groaned out loud. And began to come.

The jizzom flooded out of him in spurts—it made him groan again and ache with the delight of it. He rocked back and forth, helpless in her firm hands, her desperate, suckling mouth. He felt her swallow again and again—and then felt something else, a sudden awkwardness, a halting to the motion of her head.

As the last of his job drained out of him, Lee held himself a little distance from it by great effort and listened.

Then heard what she had seen. A soft footstep in the alley's dirt still a distance away.

The blue-eyed man had come for his robbery.

Lee pulled suddenly away, turned and stepped to the side. The girl stayed kneeling, cream still running down her chin.

The pimp stood only a few feet away—a small, slender man, looking younger than his years. His straight razor was open in his hand. The blade looked like silver in the moonlight.

Lee took the time to reach down and tuck his wet cock away. No use offering *that* for a cut. He felt a little tired, a little worn by the pleasure the One-eyed girl had given him. Not in the mood for a fight, really.

The pimp took the scene, the kneeling girl, Lee's knife, and seemed amused.

"I guess you had your fun then, John," he said. He had a hoarse hard-case's voice at odds with his slight good looks. "You hand over all your cash an' your studs and watch—we'll call it even."

"I don't suppose you're smart enough to take my word that I've got ten bucks or so left on me and not a penny more," Lee said.

The pimp smiled. "Strip and turn out," he said, "or I'll cut your throat."

The One-eyed girl moaned by the board fencing. "He's bad . . . he's a *bad* man, Harry. Be careful . . ." She sounded like an old woman, and her voice was still thick with Lee's leavings. "Oh, let him be . . ."

"You'll never," Lee said to the pimp, "get any better advice than that."

The words were hardly out of his mouth when the pimp came at him, fast as a fighting dog.

He came with the razor blade folded open across his knuckles, to swing a punch with it and hack a deep wound into Lee where it struck him.

Lee dodged away, frankly startled by the slight man's speed. The pimp moved like a man who'd done this all before, and more than once. He moved like a man who'd killed with the razor and was sure of doing it again.

Lee had seen, in Parker once, two Negroes fighting with razors, and those men had sparred and slapped out quickly—too quickly almost to see—with the blades, and soon had both been laced with fine bright lines of red. But none of the wounds deep enough to kill.

The blue-eyed pimp fought a different way entirely. He leaped in slugging, slugging with that razored fist, using his other arm only for balance as he fought.

Lee backed and backed and backed away, keeping the double-edged dagger up high between them, not trying to cut or thrust in return. If he thrust and missed, the pimp would get what he wanted—one good blow with that razor-edged fist. There would be no recovering from that damage.

No chance to recover from it. The pimp would follow it up, would slice Lee to ribbons as he staggered, bleeding to death.

The small man grunted with a near miss, spun like a dancer, and drove in again.

Lee couldn't back up forever.

And he thought now he saw a chance with this man. That relentless attack carried a weakness with it. The pimp was off balance. Swinging so hard, with all his speed and weight behind those hacking blows, the pimp was off balance for an instant as he missed.

Lee backed again, stumbling a little over some trash and the pimp was at him, jumping in, swinging hard with a grunt of expelled breath. Swinging up from his side to catch Lee across the face, to split his face like a hacked melon. Lee didn't jump back. He planted his feet, swayed back as fast as he could, like a tree struck by a furious gust of wind—felt a quick touch of ice at the side of his chin, swayed forward, caught the pimp at the extended end of his swing, and drove the broad blade of the dagger into the small man's belly.

The blade made a sudden tearing sound going in

and Lee barely got his left arm up in time to block the razor-man's backhand stroke.

The pimp drew in his breath with a whoop and jumped back, light on his feet as if Lee hadn't put seven inches of steel into his gusts. The blue-eyed man stepped back and back, keeping his fist, the open razor, high enough to guard.

When there was ten feet or so between them, the pimp looked down at himself. He was soaked from belly to foot down along that side. The blood looked black in the moonlight.

The pimp looked up at Lee. "You're a lucky fucker," he said, and started to say something more. But Lee gave him no chance—he drove the pimp as the pimp had driven for him, slashing, stabbing with the knife as he went in.

The One-eyed girl was screaming.

The pimp tried to move back, to get some room, and he was able to move. But not well. The blade had gutted him, the wound stiffening his muscles, draining the strength out of him.

Still he tried to move. He staggered back, striking out at Lee, trying for a lucky blow, trying to give Lee what Lee'd given him. A desperate, crippling wound.

He needed luck. He needed just a chance.

But his luck was out. And Lee gave him no chance at all.

He closed with the wounded man, grappled with him, and wrestled for a firm hold on the man's right arm. Held the arm and its hand that held the razor still for just an instant. Felt the pimp's slight, wiry body thrash against him—the wet of the blood soaked there—and feinted once with the knife to draw the man's left arm up high to ward it. Then swung his knife down, around, and under and drove it up into the man's belly again.

The pimp screamed a long tearing cry; the razor fell twinkling away, and Lee, with all his strength, ripped the broad blade sideways, and sliced the man open like a can of beans.

The pimp stiffened in Lee's hands and then fell kicking and clutching at his belly, trying to hold himself together. As he lay thrashing in the dirt, things forced themselves out between his gripping fingers, bulged out wetly into the moonlight.

The pimp screamed again, but tried to smother the sound he made; then he called out "*Lucy . . .!*" but the girl stayed at the fence.

As Lee stood staring down, the pimp then gritted his teeth and tried to die. His whole ruined body shook with the effort. It was as if he were trying to give birth, or already had, to the stuff squeezing out between his fingers.

Lee had had enough.

He bent over the struggling man, held his head still with one hand, and drove the point of the knife into his left eye. Lee drove the point in and leaned on the handle, and the blade grated, then slid down into the man's brain.

Lee stood up, then walked away staggering like a drunk—from tiredness, maybe, or from sickness at the pimp's hard death. A vision came up into Lee's mind like a blow; he saw Packwood struggling on all fours, shot through and through. That vision, more than this reality, made him feel so sick he leaned against the fence boards when he reached them, bent over, and retched up a bitter mouthful of vomit. He spit that out, and leaned there a while longer, trying to get his breath.

A bad, bad fight. He would then have given a great deal never to have another. The old wound in his side was hurting him, too.

"Now that was something to see."

Lee turned fast from the fence, the bloody knife ready in his hand.

Blackie stood smiling at him, a nickel plated revolver in his hand. The saloon owner looked handsomer than ever, standing in his dark evening clohes in the moonlight. The soft light shone on the gleaming white of his shirt front, sparkled off the jeweled studs.

"I was sure that Harry had you there." He shook his tom can't head. "I didn't think any man could stand up to Harry Sarseby, and him with that razor in his hand . . ." He shook his head again. "Yes, sir, something to see. Who the hell *are* you, cowboy?"

"Lucky," Lee said.

Blackie nodded, smiling. "Sure have been—up to now."

The whore had crept over to her pimp's body and was crooning to it like a mother over her sleeping child.

"Well," Lee said. "Thanks for coming out." He watched the woman for a moment, reached up and felt the blood just clotting at the side of his chin. A few inches nearer that swinging razor and it would have taken his jaw off like an ax.

"Oh, I was coming out anyway," Blackie said.

Lee noticed then that the handsome man had not put the nickel plated revolver away.

"You know," Blackie said, and he slowly stopped smiling, "old Ben Ripley came into the place tonight. Ben's not what you'd call your usual slummer. Friend of mine, really. A genuine honest man. Wine merchant, Ben is—one of the biggest." The saloon owner paused, looking up at the moon. "Now, there's a sight," he said. "Wonder how that damned thing ever got up there . . ."

He looked at Lee again, and slowly brought the revolver muzzle up to level. It was aimed at Lee's heart.

"Seems," Blackie said, "seems that some drunk cowboy—looking remarkably like you, my young friend—had the serious ill judgment to force his attentions on Adah Menckins earlier tonight. One of the girls at the theater told Ben what had happened . . ."

Lee felt a wash of cold, like icy mountain air. He stayed still, just where he was.

The handsome man was staring at him like a dark angel of judgment.

"I see . . ." Blackie said, after a moment. He seemed sad about it. "I see that that foolish cowboy was you."

Lee heard the neat click as the revolver hammer was eased back.

"Adah and I . . . well, we do back a long way. Some of this is over—some of it'll never be over." He smiled. "I'm a little old for Adah, after all." He shifted his feet slightly for better balance. "Drop that knife, cowboy. It'll do you no good at all."

Lee let the dagger fall and slowly started to back up, backing down the alley.

"No place to run down there," Blackie said, and started strolling after him, sauntering along as if nothing important were to happen.

Lee backed slowly . . . slowly, trying not to break and run, not to give the handsome man his instant reason to shoot. Back . . . slowly.

"Not the most dignified way to go, cowboy, backing away from a bullet you deserve."

Lee was alongside the tangle of telegraph wires now. He had time for one try. No more.

No use to reach for the Bisley Colt's—way too slow, back under the tail of the damned coat . . .

One try—no more.

He glanced down, picked his length of wire, stooped, got the end, whirled fifteen feet of the stuff whistling round in a great circle through the air, ducked at the flash of Blackie's pistol shot—felt the bullet burn the top of his shoulder, and sent a loop of heavy wire hissing hard enough through the air to hit the handsome man like a hammer across his face.

Blackie's cheek split from ear to chin, and blood spattered down his white shirt front. He swayed, stunned for an instant, and Lee ran for him, boots pounding in the dirt, ran to grapple him down.

And almost made it.

But not quite.

The handsome man (not so handsome now, his face ruined by that slicing blow) recovered, straightened, and Lee saw the muzzle rise again to steady on him as he charged.

Going to die. God damnit!

But there was no flash of light, no breaking blow to his chest, his head.

Instead, Blackie suddenly seemed to stretch and yawn like a man suddenly wakened, surprised. He stretched up to his full height, the revolver pointed over Lee's head. He stretched up, his mouth wide, glaring down at Lee like an avenging angel, judgment decided, then said, "Something . . . something has . . ." appeared to trip, stumbled, and fell to one knee in the dirt.

The handle of Lee's dagger stood out from Blackie's back and threw a quick moon shadow across the material of his coat.

The Chinese girl, eyes darker than shadows, stood behind him, panting.

Behind her, through a narrow streak of light where the alley door stood just ajar, Lee heard the clink and rattle of dishes, and clang of pots and pans.

"*What happened . . .?*"

Lee could hardly hear the handsome man's voice. Blackie was sitting now, in the alley dirt.

"My back feels . . . bad . . ."

Lee saw the gleaming pistol lying in the dirt past Blackie's hand. He walked up to the man. The Chinese girl watched him come; she seemed uncertain that he was pleased with her.

Lee managed to smile at her, and knelt beside the dying man.

"My Chinese girl," he said. "She picked up my knife."

Blackie lay down on his side. "That feels better," he said. He smiled up at Lee. "Do you have any idea how funny this is?" he said.

"Not yet," Lee said. "I surely don't." He wiped tears from his eyes with his coat sleeve. When he'd done that and looked again, he saw that Blackie was dead.

They went to see Seal Rock in the morning light. It was very beautiful, and the girl called out to the seals in Chinese, and laughed and clapped her hands as she watched them sporting in the sea.

Lee preferred to watch the waves. He liked the way they came crashing in, were broken, and came crashing in again. Brave and beautiful, he thought.

Better than men.

THE OTHER SIDE OF THE CANYON

ROMER ZANE GREY

THE OTHER SIDE OF THE CANYON marks the return to print of one of Zane Grey's strongest characters, Laramie Nelson, first introduced in Grey's novel RAIDERS OF SPANISH PEAKS. Laramie was a seasoned Indian fighter, an incomparable tracker, and one of the deadliest gunhands the West had ever known.

In these stories, Romer Zane Grey, son of the master storyteller, continues Laramie's adventures as he takes on a gang of train robbers, a gold thief, and a sharp-shooting woman wanted for murder!

WESTERN
0-8439
2041-6
$2.75

GUN TROUBLE IN TONTO BASIN

ROMER ZANE GREY

Gun Trouble In Tonto Basin signals the reappearance of Arizona Ames, the title character of one of Zane Grey's most memorable novels. Young Rich Ames came to lead the life of a range drifter after he participated in a gunfight that left two men dead. Ames' skill earned him a reputation as one of the fastest guns in the West.

In these splendid stories, Arizona Ames comes home to find his range and his family haunted by the shadow of a terror they dare not name!

WESTERN
0-8439-2098-X
$2.75